Fourth Reich
Reborn

A novel
by

Leisel

Original
© copyright 1999

Current
© Copyright January 2014

Fourth Reich Reborn

by

Leisel

Leiselbooks.com
visit us
BooksRinmyBlood.com

Cover Art by Laura Johnson

Fourth Reich Reborn

Adam and Gretchen Levy wake on the day of their father, Dr. Agmon Levy's funeral, only to find he was a former Nazi Hunter. The journal chronicles his life back when he was a captive in the concentration camps.
Dr. Levy leaves a trail that his children must travel-a trail that leads to the legacy of notorious Adolf Hitler!

For a list of books by this Author, go to:

Leiselbooks.com or BooksRinMyBlood.com
(For more info on the BooksRinMyBlood/Youtube series:
The 10 Things You Don't Know About:
Game of Thrones
The Harry Potter series
The 101 Dalmatians and more...

ISBN-13:978-0615975313 (Leiselbooks)
ISBN-10: 0615975313

Contents:

Fourth Reich
Reborn

Chapter 1
September 2, 2005

The sand on the Hawaiian coast looked breathtaking by
sunrise. The collage of colors made the sky look like the pink of a
salmon's belly.

The sound of the waves crashing on the rocks was nothing new
to Adam. He had lived with the sound for years, now it was
nothing more than a soft buzz on the alarm clock in his head.

Suddenly, Adam woke. His stomach turning knots, he realized
that his dad was dead. He had died the day before, and Adam
knew today was the day for his funeral. Adam shouted for his
younger sister, Gretchen, to wake. He made both of them a strong
pot of black coffee that tasted thick and had a texture like
granules of sand. He made toast with marmalade for himself but
left the other jams for Gretchen to choose, she always liked the
variety of Guava, strawberry and grape jams. He did not. It was

1

orange marmalade as far back as he could remember.

He rubbed his back, the scar was all that was left, but he rubbed it anyway.

They sat together and Adam could tell she had been crying. He knew what she was feeling, and his was an unprecedented sour taste in his gut.

"G'morning, Gretch."

"Morning. How'd you sleep? Mine was restless."

"So was mine." Adam took a deep breath, tasting the salt of the ocean on the back of his tongue. "Gretch, you've got to stop picking at your nails-look at them, they're bloody, for Christ's sake!"

Gretchen hurriedly hid her hands underneath the table. She couldn't help it-she'd been biting them since she could remember-all the way back to the womb.

Never did Adam think that his father, Agmon, would die, even though he was 68 years old when he did pass away.

Dr. Agmon Levy was a good father, he always provided for

Adam and Gretchen, always saw to their having all they needed-
especially since they moved to Hawaii fifteen years ago when
Adam was five. Adam could barely remember his mother, Lenora,
a beautiful woman of 36 when he was born- for he was only two
when death came for her during childbirth. Agmon had a
breakdown when she died and even though Adam was only five,
he knew that life would be different. And different it was, for
Agmon took the kids and moved from Arizona to Oahu, the
Hawaiian island, and set down roots.

Agmon never went to the kids soccer games and plays at the
private schools he sent them to, but he always paid the bill for
them to attend.

Adam grew to be the guiding force in his sisters life, and he
never missed when she was performing.

Adam knew someone had to be there for her, and it was him.
Adam never questioned why Agmon decided on Hawaii, he only
knew that Agmon never let the real world come into their lives,
that only living in what he considered a paradise, with the weather

3

ever the same, would do for his children.

Agmon had died the night before, peacefully in his sleep. Adam knew that his dad preferred to buried hurriedly, as did most of his Jewish faith.

They knew dad was Jewish and that their mother Lenora, though dead, was Catholic. Agmon never told anything past this- for he did not want them to cast themselves as anything other than the most decent and moral of people.

Though he was not embarrassed of his past, he never wanted it to intrude into their lives and cause pain, as he had known.

In a plain wooden box with no embalming fluid used or anything other than a Rabbi present, Adam and Gretchen lay their father down in the Jewish section of the cemetery, repeating phrases in in accordance with the Rabbi until it was done.

After the service the Rabbi spoke.

"I know that when your father was alive he was a great man. A great man, indeed. I did not know Agmon was living in Hawaii."

Adam spoke as he touched the yarmulke on his head, "We

4

really don't even know what he did do. He never liked to talk about it much."

"What? He was the great man, Dr. Agmon Levy, am I correct?"

"Yes, but we don't know what you mean by 'great'?"

"This man, Agmon was of great service to his people-he was a prisoner in a concentration camp for months! He escaped, and helped the Nation of Israel track down and put war criminals to justice. How do you not know this? Did your father never mention it?" the Rabbi asked furiously.

"Ahh, no, I don't think so." Gretchen said, "Or he would have told us. Our mother, Lenora was a Catholic and he never had us even declare a religion. He only wanted us to be decent people, like he was. He led us by example."

"Feh! There was a big part of the Doctors life that he never told you two about- I suggest that you look him up. Use the internet, I did! See what he was famous for-I cannot believe that you two would have nothing to say. Check with Mossad; see

5

what your father accomplished. Shalom to both of you-may God bless and watch over you." The Rabbi said as he walked fuming out of the cemetery.

"What was that all about?" Gretchen asked.

"I don't even know." Adam answered. "But I think there's a whole story there, somewhere."
Adam reassured her and put his arm around her shoulders as they began to walk.

"You know," Adam began, "we're it now. We're all that's left. There's no aunt's, uncles, or cousins. When dad died, he left just the two of us."

Gretchen sighed. Then, "I know, I've been thinking about it awhile now. Not specifically about dad dying, but about why we're here; you know, life and death? Like for instance, what are you afraid of, Adam?"

"Heights, mostly. But there's not a whole lot of need to worry about that, here in Hawaii" He said softly.

"Oy! Fercockt-that's what that is!" Gretchen liked the Yiddish

6

cussing that she had heard dad used, and tried to use it now.

"Heights!? How would you even know that? You've never been higher than Diamond Head."

"Gretch! Watch your mouth, today of all days- I simply meant that I *am* afraid of some things. Oh, what the hell! You wouldn't understand." he said.

"I think I do understand, more than you know. I know why you never had a serious girlfriend, because your fear of rejection. But I'm telling you that since you've grown up, since you healed, which was years ago, you're a real hotie! I'm serious. You have nothing to be embarrassed about anymore. There! I said it." Gretch said with a wink. "You know what I'm afraid of?"

"That your taking psychology classes was a waste of time?"

"Death." And with that she became serious once again.

"I think it's okay for you to think about that today, because of dad's dying; but after today I don't want to hear one more word out of you, okay? No more talk about death and dying!" then he ran his fingers through her long blonde- honey colored hair, pushing her head down in a friendly, brotherly way.

Coming back to the house they went through all the papers in their dad's library.

"I went through dad's important papers, life insurance stuff, what to do with the death certificates, when we get them. All necessary stuff, but I didn't find anything about his life. My guess is that all that information is at his safe deposit box, what do you think?" Adam said as he held up a key from the local bank.

"I think you're right. I'm going to do what the Rabbi suggested, I'm going to look up Agmon Levy, and what he did to become, as the Rabbi said, 'A great man!'" she laughed in a way that would make you think that she wouldn't find anything. After all, her dad was just that-her dad. Certainly he didn't have a past that would make him 'great', not *her* dad. She was curiously intent on finding out.

Several hours after Adam and Gretchen were finished talking, Gretchen yelled from her bedroom, "Adam! Come quick, you have got to see this."

8

Adam ran into her room and saw her with her laptop, open and on a web-page from the Israeli Intelligence agency. Gretchen was almost catatonic.

"What is it? What's happened?" Adam asked.

"I was searching Agmon's name, and it came up under the Israeli Intelligence page! And look closer, it's under the MOSSAD agency- up until last year MOSSAD had it covered up, nobody knew anything about them. But now they've uncovered some names from the past, men and women who they're grateful for, and one of them was Dr. AGMON LEVY!" she sounded so excited, she couldn't get it out fast enough.

"What is *MOSSAD?*" Adam asked.

"It says it was the agency that followed the tracks of the war criminals, the SS, SA, all the people who committed crimes against humanity by running concentration camps. I mean this is *big*! I can't believe that dad would have been involved in this at all. He was so docile, so quiet all the time-I can't see him tracking down Nazi's for a living. But you remember what that Rabbi said?

9

He said that he was a great man, why would he have said it if it wasn't true?"

"I can't believe it, either." Adam said with the most curious look. "This is crazy, surely we would have had some kind of warning if this were the truth. A man can't just jump out of the pages of history and turn out that he was your dad!"

"I don't believe it." Adam resoundingly said, "It can't be dad, *it just can't!"* his hands unfolded and he had started to unravel his worn out t-shirt.

Adam started pacing, finally he said, "I've gone through dad's things here, all the papers he wanted us to have. Life insurance papers, and such. But there was also a key, I'll bet it was to a safe deposit box, which I'm sure just had more of the same. But, what if it had more information on this, what *if* there were more?"

Adam and Gretchen looked excitedly at each other. Adam said, "We're going to find out! Grab your flip-flops; we're going to the bank right after we stop by the lawyers."

And out the door they flew on a warm Oahu afternoon.

Chapter 2

When they were at the lawyers office, Mr. Navski said the

following, "Well, no big secrets here; Agmon left everything to

you both, Adam and Gretchen. It's a general will, easy enough.

Looks like your both going to be well off for decades to come."

Adam was satisfied with what he said but added, "I want to be

certain, for Gretchen's future mainly. But how much is 'well off'?"

"About 20 million for each of you. Taxes are already paid for,

he thought of everything. That, plus the house, which is about 8

million. Is that well off enough for you?" the lawyer laughed a

deep chuckle. "My fees have already been paid as well, so is there

anything else I can do for you?"

"How about the name of a good financial planner?" Adam

joked back, but his head was reeling. He knew his dad had

prepaid his admission to the Hawaii Pacific University, no matter

how long his program continued. Getting his MBA with his core

on finance was still a pipe-dream to Adam, but he had a 4.0

grade-average and had no idea to start slowing down. He had graduated from the University and was now in his first year to getting his MBA. He still had at least one more year of school to go.

Gretchen had just graduated from High School and her tuition had been paid for as well, no matter what she wanted to major in, but she had a feeling she wanted to go into the medical field, maybe becoming a doctor like her father had been.

"I'm happy that at least got to graduate high school before dad passed. I know it was really important to him that I get my education." Gretchen said solemnly.

"I just wish I had finished the University before he died because I know he wanted that education for me more than he wanted anything for me. I couldn't do that for him." Adam said as they both walked out of the lawyers office and into the remaining rays of the afternoon. A brisk rainshower had just missed them while they were in talking to the lawyer. The air smelled clean with a hint of hibiscus flowers and sand.

"Don't go beating yourself about that." Gretchen said as she pulled Adam's arm. "You don't get to decide when we die, only God does that."

Adam nodded his head slowly. "You're right. I guess I just miss him; that's all."

"We *both* miss him. Remember that."

Chapter 3

Adam and Gretchen arrived at the bank, supplied with their key, and they were surprised when they opened the safety deposit box. They were alone in the room and it was silent. Inside was a ton of cash, much more than they would have expected, if they expected any at all. Adam already knew that their dad left them the property on which their house resided, knew about the life insurance he had taken out on not only himself but his precious wife Lenora. Agmon was a rich man, much more than Adam could have guessed. For though they lived in Oahu and went to private schools, they never had a *rich* lifestyle.

Adam had taken up surfing, a daily passion- but nothing more than that. The fact that Agmon had told them that he expected them both to educate themselves with a university education that had been paid for in advance they took for granted. They both knew that their lives would go through the University of Hawaii before it would take them anywhere else.

Adam had knew now that he and Gretchen were rich-with

sums of 20 million dollars each, and the house which was a beautiful Hawaiian mansion with manicured lawns that led down to the sea, it seemed that Agmon left them a few more stacks of cash and a map of their property, marked with a big, black **X,** under the garden in the backyard.

"What is this supposed to be, Adam?" Gretchen said obviously taken back with amazement.

"I don't know, Gretch. I don't know." Adam said with equal shock. They continued to stand in the bank vault, readily taking their time for the elderly bank president them they could have all the time they needed. He was also acquainted with Agmon Levy, and told Adam and Gretchen so, he gave them his condolences.

Underneath the money was a journal, and a note from Agmon to his kids. It read,

My dearest children;

At last I am dead, and by now, buried. I have this money from investments and such that paid off well. I have saved it for you, as I could never be happy since my dearest Lenora was taken from

me. By now I am with her in the beyond, and I will find my

happiness once more.

I have also included my journals I kept since I escaped the

Buchenwald concentration camp. I know these were tragic times

and that's precisely why I kept them from you. When I fell in love

with Lenora I felt a lightness in my soul that I never thought I

could feel again. This turned to the deepest love when you born,

Adam. Then, when she was pregnant once again I thought I could

never feel all the love in the universe- that it was too much-I felt

that it could not last. I was right... for Lenora died in childbirth,

and it all fell away in a flash! I didn't feel anything- but I DID

love you both immensely. I packed our bags and moved to

Hawaii- the farthest place in the world from the concentration

camps I could think of. I am not a fool, but I knew that I would

never feel love again, and I wanted the both of you to have a

good life, and I knew you could if I isolated your lives with what I

considered paradise.

At least now I'm sure you'll do right by using the money I left *for you to find happiness. Use it well. Take it as **payment in full**.*

Read my journals only if you want to know the wretched life I

lived.

    To this day I miss my father, mother and my little sister,

Sara, who perished in the gas chambers at Buchenwald. A part

of me died that day as well, but I am glad to know I leave you

behind. Remember, you can only make the world a better place by

the ones you leave behind. I leave you, so I leave the world a

better place.

Love to you, my dear children,

 Agmon

p.s. Dig under the X, approximately 6 feet. There is a surprise for

you both underneath the garden.

Adam and Gretchen stood there staring at the letter. Gretchen

said, "Can I keep it? Please? The letter I mean, not the money."

"Yeah, sure you can." Adam pulled the journals out of the box

and said, "If I can keep the journals. I think that dad meant for me

to read them."

"What are we going to do with the money? Keep it here? Maybe we should open another account or, I don't know." Gretchen started to cry and turned to Adam's chest to bury her face. Adam put his arms around her, knowing that from now on his role as big brother he would take more seriously.

Adam decided to keep the money in the safe deposit box as Agmon had paid for it for two more years. He folded the map and put it in his pocket to use when they got home. He was also certain that he would take the journals to read as the stars came out.

The next day Adam started to dig up the flower bed under the bedroom of the late Agmon. It wasn't until late that afternoon when he struck the top of a huge chemical barrel.

He called Gretchen over, "Are you ready?"

"Let's do it!"

He lifted the lid slowly and there started to shine was the deep golden color of 200 bars of gold, at least 100 million dollars!

Gretchen fell to the ground, aghast. "I don't understand. He's already left us more money than we can use. What the hell?"

Adam took the handkerchief out of his back pocket and ran it over his forehead.

"He said we would find a surprise. I guess this is us-surprised." he said, "I say we bury it until we know what this is about, what do you think?"

"Cover it up."

Chapter 4

Late into the night Adam kept reading through the journals. He was captivated by the horror he read and didn't know how his dad had survived. Yes, he knew that his father's family had lived in a tiny village near Wiemar, Germany when World War II had broken out, how his grandfather had volunteered for the German army but gave away their secret; that they were Jewish. German, yes- but Jewish nonetheless. He continued to read:

My father and mother and sister and I were taken by a train to the Buchenwald concentration camp, and were each given numbers we had tattooed on our arms. We were now living in bunkhouses and my father was sent during the day for work detail. They dug for days, a hole that was about six km deep and about 50 mm long. We could not figure out what it was for, but he kept digging. Then on about the third day we found out what they were for- for then it was that a group of homosexuals, cripples, and Negroes were lined up with their hands tied up, then shot in the back with pistols. They fell like cords of wood into the pre-dug trench. I will never forget the sound of the thud their bodies made when they fell into the open graves.

But we never thought they would do that to us- we were only Jewish, surely the country did not have issue with us-we were only Jewish!

But then after we saw group after group killed in that fashion we became scared for our own safety. We had lived in fear for months now, and early one day the soldiers marched us out of the bunkhouses and onto the line leading into the chamber. Some of the women were crying as were their children. It all seemed so unreal. We were already starving to death, surely they would leave us alone. But they continued to line us up, in our striped convict shreds- for the last time. They were no more than unsympathetic shields against the cold. My father tried to keep us together, but the soldiers were stern and had no sympathy for us, and we were all pushed, striped naked, into a huge shower, or so we thought. There were shower heads above, but then instead of *water, a seeping sound filled the air. There were sounds of crying as mothers held their babies lifeless in their hands. The cries got louder and my fear gripped my stomach, for I knew what was next.*

One by one the bodies fell, and the noise from the many inside became an even more ominous quiet. Our group was not immune, for one by one we all fell silent. My little sister, Sara, fell first. Her limp little body was tragic to see, my mother was next. She looked at me with a pleading she did not have voice, she looked at me until she died. My father was next-strong and proud he was going to lead his family in the next life, since he had failed in this one.

I was the only one left- I don't know how or why-but I fell with my eyes open, ready to die. I must have passed out for the fear let go my stomach. When I woke I was in a pile of bodies, but I dared not move for they would see my movements. I lay there all day into the night. When I tried to move I did not dare look around for fear of seeing my family. I could not bare to see them

22

like this. I crawled out of the pile and crawled into a little space

under the fence-only when I got there I was grabbed by the

shoulders and I thought it was a German soldier, but it was not.

There on the ground was the man who would mold the rest of my

life- Adam Rosenstein. He kept me from being electrocuted by the

electric fence that I had no way of knowing about. He saved my

life in more ways than one. He said that we would have to crawl

to the back entrance where the fence wasn't turned on. We got

out, I don't know how, but we got out.

Then we managed to get help getting out of Germany with the

underground pipeline that a system of Germans both Jewish and

non-Jewish had set up to get people out of the country. I owe that

man my life,and if I ever have a son I will name him after Adam.

When we were both safe and fed we decided to do something,

we decided to help people around the world understand that the

Germans were doing this unthinkable atrocity not only to Jewish

people, but to all useless people in the German's eye's.

The world took it's time to recognize the horrors that were being committed right under their noses but eventually got behind us

and we joined the Israeli Intelligence agency- the MOSSAD

division. I wanted go even deeper than MOSSAD, and I finally,

after 20 years, made it into the most secret of ranks- to this day I

cannot even write down their name.

There we were able to others capturing Nazi criminals over

the world, the scum! They scattered like vermin when the days of

war were soon over. None of them had the honor and strength to

stand up and be counted at the end. Cowards!

Norway, Brazil, Argentina...and more; these were the

countries that the vermin scattered, but Adam and I could smell

them right away. Eichmann was a big rat, he tried to hide, but we

got him after all. He cried that he was innocent, that he was not

Eichmann, but fingerprints, ah! Yes, a man cannot change his

fingerprints. At least that's what we thought. After Eichmann was

captured there were men who attempted changing their fingertips

with dead mens- who knows if they were dead already or if they

only knew death after meeting these wretched men.

24

How does a man attempt to steal another man's life?

Sometimes when they took another man's fingertips, they took his whole hand, then carefully sliced the man's prints onto their already waiting fingers, sliced down to the millimeter, waiting for the new skin to heal. We knew these men right away-hands with the oval scabs, what a sorry way for these unfortunate men, the original owners to wind up-with their hands cut off.

But there was one man I have never forgotten.
One man with whom I put the whole Nazi regimes trust into.

Adolf Hitler. History says that Hitler died that day in April, in 1945. I say different. Hitler had a god complex, a feeling that he was the chosen one- I do not buy that he committed suicide, I do not believe that Eva Braun went with him to end of her life. I believe that he had his double take the fall, had him killed then burned. Same for Eva. After they married April 29, 1945, why would they take their lives? No. they got away with nothing! I have been chasing Hitler ever since I woke up with the dead bodies of my family all around me! How can I express the horror

25

of that time? No, I believe that Hitler is alive to this day, living

his days with Eva and evil thugs who still follow him.

Adam fell asleep with the journals as his pillows-captivated by

whom his father really was-a champion for the Jewish people.

Not only the Jewish people, but for the underdogs who died at the

hands of Hitler who took it upon himself to murder, some say, 16

million over the course of the Third Reich.

Chapter 5

April 27, 1945

The last days of the war had arrived. All hope gone, Adolf Hitler was sullen. He stared at the large wooden map he used for strategical reasons. He was spent. Never did he think it would end up like this. Adolf twirled a thread that was unraveling from his uniform jacket, then he left it there. The medals on his uniform were rusty, despite the efforts of Linge, Hitler's valet. Linge would to anything for the Führer, even spend the last days of war underground in the bunker. Linge was an old man, but not too old. He remembered the old days of Germany, he remembered when he was a boy, when things were good for Germany. He reminisced how Germany was made to crawl on it's knees and beg for food- for it's existence.

The world had taken it's pound of flesh for starting the first World War, right out of the German peoples mouths.

Linge hated that world. Now, here was Hitler, what a god he was in Linges' eyes. He served Hitler with all the fervor in his soul.

The bombs were exploding louder and more closely together, like thunderclaps bringing the storm close by. Hitler was nervous, but he pretended to be strong in front of the men and women in the bunker.

"The Russians are right on our doorstep, but they will never get close enough! I will show them, the bastards! They will never get to me, never!" Hitler shouted, with the frothing at the mouth that had been quite usual for some time.

"What are you saying, mein Führer?" Joseph Goebbels asked with a cowardly strain in his voice.

soul. Linge never stepped more than a few yards away from Hitler, even when he said he was going underground, literally. Hitler's plans were to go to the Führerbunker, an underground concrete bunker that could survive the expected strike of the Russians.

Adolf stood waving his fist in the air, as he so often did, "What I have been saying all along. I will not have my body put on

28

public display! To have those leeches spit on my grave, NO! Those Russian cowards would love to hang my body in some kind of circus freak show, as they did with that slimy turn coat, Mussolini! Hung him upside down and spat on him! I will not have it!" Images of Mussolini were going through his mind, as he pounded on the wooden table as if that would stop the war.

"How do you plan to stop them, mein Führer?" Goebbels asked.

"I will see them in *Holle*! I will kill myself before I let them touch my body. Yes, kill myself then have the guards burn my body to ashes."

Adolf turned silent, as did everyone in the bunker. The thought turned to what the world would be like without Adolf Hitler, and they did *not* like what they saw.

Suddenly the guards led the way into the room accompanied by Eva Braun. Eva was young and strong, even for a woman, and (unforgivably Hitler). Of course she had her doubts about the Third Reich, but if Adolf could dream it, then so must it be. She had followed him to the bunker to show her support, plus she had a secret agenda.

More than anything, she wanted to become his wife. She knew the world hardly even knew of her, but she also knew when the war was over, historians would study Hitler, and she would become a footnote, merely a bystander in Hitler's life. She wasn't going to go out as his mistress!

She arrived dressed so beautifully in the blue frock Adolf had bought for her. The hard job was *not* for Eva to be so breathtaking in the bunker, the men had been down there for weeks. Any woman dressed that way would have been a breath of fresh air.

"Was ist loss?" Hitler said quietly, as she marched down to his side.

Hitler took a small breath, this stunning woman was his. "What have we here?"

Eva smiled. She knew she had cast upon him her certain spell.

He can rule the world, but I will rule him.

With a rush, Adolf was upon her, taking her to a back room.

"Eva," he began, "My dear Eva. Why have you come here? I thought I had put you in the Berghof for your own protection. Why would you come here, why Eva, why?"

"My dear Adolf," Eva began, "How could I stay away?" When I did not know what was to become of you? You know how slowly it takes messages to travel these days- don't you know what they are saying about you? About the Third Reich? They are saying horrid things, about you and the Jewish people. They are saying you, Adolf, *you* gave the order to murder thousands, maybe even millions..."

"Enough!" Adolf shouted. "Enough, I say. I will not discuss politics with a woman! Anything that is said is being said by my enemies are lies! Enough said!"he grabbed her by the throat.

Eva's heart sank. She had wanted him to propose marriage to her, and now he was angry. She shyly touched his ear, then ran her finger down the side of his face.

"I am sorry I tried to talk to you about politics. You are absolutely right, a woman has no business talking about what she does not understand. I do not want to make you angry with me, Schatzi. All I want to do is to make you happy, that's why I came to the bunker. Please do not be angry with me." Then she tried to pull the corners of his lips into a smile. She failed.

Adolf was unhappy, but not with her. Adolf pulled her close to his side.

"I do not care what is being said," Adolf began,

"It is all hopeless. I do not care about the war, I do not care about anything. Except for you, Eva."

Adolf pulled her close and she thought she felt sobs. That could not be.

"What do you mean, Adolf?" Eva whispered. She could feel his limp body against hers.

"I mean I want to marry you, Eva."

Finally! Eva could feel his body shaking as she held him up. He was shaking quite a bit these days, although he tried to hide it by putting his hands in his pockets. His hands shook so much lately. She had often wondered why in these last days he had stopped making appearances, why he had only let certain film footage of himself be released. He looked tired, and dirty. *The filth of living in the bunker.* But no! He looked fat, worse than tired. He looked old.

So much had been on his mind lately... Eva tried to tell herself that was the reason he looked the way he did, and yet she was not certain. Eva knew that their relationship was a mystery to those who knew Adolf best. She knew that everyone wondered what they did when they were alone.

Well, it is none of their business. She shuddered when she thought of it. *He is a sick, immoral man, but he is _my_ immoral man. And no one will take him from me!*

"I have always said that Germany was my bride, but I am ready for you to take it's place in my heart." Adolf said as he took her hands.

Eva was trembling. She nervously said, "Ja!"

"But Adolf," Eva began, "When shall we get married? I do not want to wait very long..."

Adolf cut her off, "Shh, Eva. I do not want to wait either. We shall be married right here, as soon as possible."

Eva shook from head to toe. This was too wonderful for words. Eva was to become the wife of the Chancellor, the Führer. This meant so much to the woman who had knowledge of some of the most heinous crimes in history, but her lust for notoriety and power overlooked the events that would haunt mankind forever.

Chapter 6

The following days were special as Eva made all the preparations for the wedding.

Albert Speer made an appearance, but for no more than a day. Speer and Hitler spoke in the solitude of the führer-bunker.

"I regret to tell you about the troops, they are all leaving. There is nothing more I can do, mein Führer." he snapped his heels together and made an effort to be as official as possible, here at the end.

Hitler looked ahead, staring straight at the concrete wall. Then Hitler made his wishes known, for he did not want to go out like the Italians under Mussolini.

"I will do my best to get word out to the last fighting man, mein Führer." and he clicked his heels again, then left Hitler staring at the wall.

They made sure that Walter Wagner would be there, Gauleiter of Berlin, to perform the ceremony, although it was very hushed. Even Fraü Junge, Hitler's secretary, didn't know why they had called him.

"Vhy did you call Herr Gauleiter? Vhat do you vant with him?"
Fraü Junge questioned Eva with her strong German tone.

"Oh," said Eva, "All will be evident very soon." Eva said in
flippant voice.

"You do *not* think, do you, that the Führer will marry you?" Fraü
Junge laughed a nasty laugh.

"We will see." Eva chuckled to herself.

All was finally ready on April 29th, 1945 in the
map room, in the bunker. They had asked Martin Boorman and
Joseph Goebbels to be witnesses.

Hitler's secretaries wept, except for Fraü Junge, who looked
annoyed.

Joseph Goebbels children, all six of them stood around smiling
and giddy. The baby slept quietly in the corner. There was
Helmut, Helga, Heide, Hedda, Holda and Hilde.

"I can not believe it, Father," Helmut stated, "Our Führer is
getting married!"

"I can not believe it either!" Helga said.

"Ja," Joseph Goebbels said, "Now be still, our Führer has been most generous in letting us take part in his wedding."

"And you get to be one of the witnesses," Holde blurted out, "I could just die, papa, I could just die!"

That sentence gripped Joseph Goebbels in the stomach. He began to sob quietly.

'Ja,' he thought, 'you will die. And myself also.'

This plan that Hitler had come up with struck at Goebbels heart. He had already said that his family would kill themselves to go along with Hitler's plans. The thought of them all being so happy now, only to die by their own hands later was a nauseating thought.

They married quietly.

Fraü Junge was unhappy with the way things had turned out. She had always thought of the Führer as being something of a god. This made him a mortal to her. Then there was the thought of Eva Braun becoming his wife.

Perhaps it was just the normal friction between woman, but she didn't like Eva. She had discussed

this before with Magda Goebbels, Josephs wife.

"This marriage between them is disgusting." Fraü Junge spat. "She is swine!"

"Ja," Magda began, "so ordinary, so common of her to come down to the bunker, and make him marry her."

"There is nothing we can do about it, you know that."

"I know." Magda sulked.

There was nothing they could do, except get ready for the wedding and attend, and try to look happy. However, Fraü Junge thought of the overshadowing suicide, and she wondered how much, if anything, Eva knew.

Fraü Junge was wise when she thought Eva knew nothing of the suicides to come. Eva was spellbound with happiness.

"Oh Adolf," Eva began, "I am *so* happy! I wonder where we will start our life together. Maybe we could get away to South America- I hear that many of our comrades have gone to South

America, their leader, Juan Peron seems to be so welcoming to our people. I wonder..."

Adolf cut her off, "No, no Eva. Our lives will start together by ending. We will start our lives in the hereafter. I have already made plans to commit suicide on the night of the Sabbath for witches. Walpurgisnacht night, tomorrow night. And you my dear, will join me." He held out his hand open palmed to her. She reluctantly put her hand in his.

Eva started trembling. He couldn't mean it. How could they start their future by ending it all?

"But, Adolf..." Eva started saying between tears, "You do *not* mean that, do you? I mean, I did not come here to die. I was hoping you could take me with you, I want to *live,* my shatz. I do not want to die."

Adolf thought about what she had said. He shook is head, and with his shaky hand started to flip one of her curls around his finger.

"I know what is best. You do not know, as I do, what those

Russian bastards would do to me. You don't know how badly they want to get their hands on me." he shook violently.

"I know how happy you have made me," Eva said softly, "That is all I know. You are the Führer, if you wanted to get away you could do it. You could get your double, what's his name..."

"Gustav Velar," Adolf replied.

"Ja, that's him. You could get Gustav to die in your place, nobody has to know it was him. The dental records are switched easily enough. Oh, please Adolf. Consider this."

Chapter 7

Adolf apparently did give consideration to her idea. For in the following hour he gave orders to bring Gustav Velar to him. Still he had not told his minions of his change in plans.

Joseph Goebbels was still depressed about the upcoming suicides, for the plan was when Hitler was dead, he and his wife Magda and their seven children would follow, even the baby that kept on crying.

Suddenly, Hitler seemed to be in great spirits.

"You will all join me and dance if it were their last dance on Earth!"

"A dance?" Fraü Junge commented.

"Ja. I want you all to join in. I feel like living today!" Hitler shouted.

Fraü Junge was surprised by the Führer's good spirits, but she was happy to see him in such a good mood. She made the arrangements of getting music together, and something festive to drink.

41

Martin Boorman helped her, but seemed to have a lot on his shoulders. When you considered what he was planning after the fall of the Third Reich, you wondered how he managed to keep it quiet.

Boorman planed on getting out alive. Even if he had to surrender to the Russians, so be it.

Linz, Hitler's valet, also had getting out alive on his mind. Linz was loyal to the Führer, but about when one thinks *of* ones self?

He did not plan on dying down there. Linz kept his mind busy on placing decorations for the dance. Decorations, hah! They had been down in that bunker for so long that anything was decorative. Even old paint cans with pieces of torn map intertwined seemed festive.

The dance was as festive as any Oktoberfest they could remember. They all danced, drank, and told old war stories to each other until they passed out. The bunker smelled of tobacco and human sweat, to the point of tasting the sewage when you swallowed.

"Adolf," Eva said, "Have you given thought to what I mentioned last night?"

Adolf smiled at little smile. He pulled Eva down onto his lap and whispered, "Yes, my shatz. I have given much thought to your suggestion, and I have decided that we will start our lives together with hope. Hope for another Reich, and hope for mankind. But, you will *not* tell anyone. Absolutely no one."

Eva was elated. She curled her toes in her shoes.

Yes, this was Adolf that she loved. She began to cry.

Fraü Junge saw her and thought, *Hmm, I guess the Führer has told her of the suicides. Good. That will teach her a thing or two.*

Later that night, Hitler called a meeting with Linge. Except for the occasional bombs, it was eerily silent.

"Linge," Adolf began, "I have called you here because I have to do what is most important to me. I do not want this to go any further, I do not want any talk."

"Ja, mein Führer. You can trust me, I am your humble servant."

43

Linge said with sincerity.

"This is how you will make it happen. I will make it look like I committed suicide, but I will kill Veler in my place. I will then go with the pilot who offered to take me away before, but I had refused him. I will not tell you where I am to go, for if they find out this plot, they will kill you to find out its consequences."

Linge was shocked. He knew the Führer meant it, but he could not mean that he was going to abandon them. He became dizzy and had to find a place to sit.

"No, mein Führer! No! You can not leave us here to die. What about the Aryan race? What about those Jewish saukerls? You can *not* mean you would leave us *here*, to *die*?"

Adolf's face twisted into rage. "I did not say I was going to leave you here to be taken advantage of by the Russian spurians! I will lay low for a short time, then when they are off my back, I will form a new government! A better government, with strong generals unafraid to take on the world. Not like those weak kneed slothful bastards I have now. No! I will find men with fortitude,

44

who won't back down." He brought his fist down on the table with a loud boom.

Linge felt only a little better then. He walked away, making the plans for the phony suicide.

Eva was off in her room, packing her dresses and planning on leaving behind some of her jewelry to the secretaries. Fraü Junge came to her door, and knocked a rather dull knock.

"It is me, Fraülein Braun."

"It's Fraü Hitler now." Eva said.

"Why are you packing? Surely you do not need clothes in the afterlife."

"I am doing it because I choose to keep my things neat, and I do not think I can change that now."

"I saw you crying last night," Fraü Junge said, looking for clues that would give Eva away.

"Oh?" said Eva, "I was crying because my heart is filled with joy."

45

"How could you be happy when the Führer must have told you about the suicides? Surely that could not have been the case?"

"Fraü Junge," Eva said firmly, "Vhy is it that I feel that you are always vatching me? Vhat exactly is on your mind?"

"It is no secret that I have always thought of the Führer as a god. Then you come along, and now suddenly I have to vatch the god become a silly man. It is vile, I tell you; vile and ghastly!"

It became evident that Fraü Junge had been drinking, she became clumsy, and toppled over on of Eva's suitcases. Then she stood up with as much command presence as she could muster.

"No!" Eva shouted back, "it is not vile! I love him, more than I have ever loved any man."

"Huh!" Fraü Junge snickered, "he is the *only* man you have ever loved. The only man in which you could dig your claws! Do not try to tell me otherwise, I went through your dossier months ago, you are but a child to him."

Eva knew she was right. But she also knew she was now Fraü

Hitler, and she would not have to put up with her insults.

"I think this conversation has gone on long enough, and you had better get along with your duties or I will have to..."

"You will have to vhat? Is this the new Fraü Hitler trying to flex her muscles? Ha!"

Eva lunged at her, hitting her with both fists.

Fraü Junge was no beginner to cat fights, and had Eva on the floor in seconds. Eva yelled, the men separated them in seconds.

"Break it up!" Martin Boorman yelled.

"Vhat is the meaning of this?" Adolf asked Eva.

"Fraü Junge and I were having a discussion, one that got out of control." Eva said as she smoothed her hair back into place.

"Is this true, Fraü Junge?" Adolf asked.

"Ja, it is true, mein Führer. I hope you can forgive me. I have been under a lot of stress, living in this bunker."

It was quite evident to everyone that Frau Junge had been drinking. Her hair was a mess, and her blouse pulled up, and she didn't even try to fix them.

47

"Right, then," Adolf said, "Eva, you come vith me."

"I need to give the cook some last minute instructions, Shatz...I will come immediately after." And off Eva went.

Hitler made haste to take the pills that Linge had laid out for him. Red, green, blue... there were so many, and now Eva would have to give them to him. It never occurred to Hitler that he was what would now be considered a junkie. It was considered a healthy habit when the doctor prescribed him just one pill after another. Pills were for his shaky hands, which had now become a shaky head as well.

He remembered how not ago he had awakened with stomach pains. He remembered how the doctor who appeared had called the pills he was taking 'poison'. The doctor had called the name 'strychnine,' and though he wasn't sure what that was, he had the doctor sent away and had labeled him a quack.

Adolf took a moment to gaze fondly at the picture of his mother. It has been said that he respected his father, but loved his mother.

His mother, Klara Hitler, had two still births before him, and therefore loved him to the point of smothering. With his sister Paula, who was born after him, Adolf was raised in a normal lower-middle-class household

It was often said, if not quietly, that he was part Jewish, for his mother worked for a Jewish man. Those were rumors Adolf hated to hear.

Later, when his father died, and then his mother as well, he lived on a small inheritance while he pursued art. He was good at it, but could not make his living at it, which to be sure would be the failing of the society that produced him.

There were also rumors that a Jewish man ran the art store where Hitler sold his paintings, but soon turned him away. Hitler gave it one last try, but failed to get into the Academy of Fine Arts. They said his portraits were not lifelike enough.

It was during this time that he came into contact with a Jewish prostitute who gave him syphilis, another reason to hate the Jews.

Adolf tried to escape the draft for the First World War, but

49

eventually he gave up and for reasons known only to him, enlisted in the Army. No one knew why he joined, but he made up for it when he did join. Hitler was decorated with the Silver Cross for bravery.

Adolf kept to himself. Moody, tense...he spoke in short sentences, and when he did speak he did so only making racist remarks and tried to blame the worlds woes on Jews. He started to get other men to join him, especially when he would show them pamphlets that he had picked up in town. Pamphlets that showed Jewish men, grotesquely drawn, raping young, nubile Aryan women. Pictures of Jewish men hoarding the money the from the banks. Yes, he was a man of few words, but a picture was worth a thousand of them.

Eva brought him back to the present.

"Shatzi?" Eva said as she walked up behind him. "I was wondering where you were hiding. I only now decided to check in here."

"Oh, Eva." Hitler spoke softly, "Do you think ve are doing

right to leave everyone here as we go off to start our new life? I was talking with Linge, he makes me feel as if I were abandoning him. And so too, the others."

Eva had only to think of Fraü Junge.

"You forget," Eva said, "You are god! You have the right to do vhatever you please. If that means leaving a few little people behind to clean up the mess, then so shall it be!"

God. She had said it. Often Hitler thought of himself as God. He would often stare in wonder as the people would line up like sheep to do his bidding.

Of course, she was right. Because she made him right. Eva had become warmer as she spoke. She had only realized the room they were in was a damp, dark little room.

There was a small couch and a light hung from the ceiling. The stench was from well worn boots, along with mildewed wool from the uniforms and rotting bricks. The light was the only illumination in the room, and it swung back and forth along with the bombs outside. There was a small leak in the corner of

51

the room, adding to that dank odor. Adolf seemed to take it all in stride, but Eva could not.

"Adolf," she began, "Let us hurry. I cannot take much more of this."

Adolf thought about it for a moment. Of course she was not used to this rotten bunker, no wife of the Führer should have to get used to it, either.

"Do not vorry, my darling." Adolf began, "I have already made plans to leave tonight."

"Oh! I will finish packing right away."

"No!" Adolf shouted under his breath. "Absolutely not." He walked up to Eva, then gently said in her ear, "ve cannot make it look like we are leaving. It has to look like we committed suicide. I will have my most trusted men burn the bodies when it is over. There are some people here I do not trust. They must believe I died, do you understand?"

Eva nodded her head.

"Good, we cannot take anything with us. Ve vill leave about

the same time as I murder my double. Ve vill leave with my most trusted pilot, and ve vill not look back."

Eva understood. She was nervous, but thrilled that she had talked Adolf into having a new life. Eva wasn't sure who it was that Adolf couldn't trust, so she kept quiet. She was also sure that she was being watched, so just in case, she gave her most precious jewels to one of the secretaries.

Time was running out. Eva went with Adolf into one of the small rooms in the bunker, and he gave orders not to bother them until after a shot was heard, indicating that the deed was done.

The secretaries and Fraü Junge were all crying in the kitchen, and Magda and Joseph Goebbels were readying the demise of their own children, then themselves.

They had discussed all: they would wait until the children had gone to sleep with the potion they had concocted, then give them arsenic. Magda had been drinking all afternoon, and was hardly in a state to accomplish what they had planned.

But still they waited. Until Magda could wait no longer. She went ahead and started putting the plan in motion.

Back in the anteroom stood Hitler, Eva,Velar(dead, shot through the head by Hitler), and a woman of unknown origin who resembled Eve(also dead). They had planned to get out the back way, and get to the waiting plane. Very carefully they hurried down the back hallway when they ran into Joseph Goebbels.

"Mein Führer!" He almost yelled. Joseph was shocked indeed. "My wife has dealt with my children my darling children, and is ready to kill herself. I wonder why you are not doing the same?"

"Joseph," Adolf whispered, "come with us. I promise we will start anew. Come now!"

"But as I already told you, my wife, my children…"

"There is only room for one more. Come if you would like, but otherwise say nothing of this meeting. It does not matter to me. Ve vill go now."

Adolf and Eva started scurrying down the hall.
Joseph had to make his decision quickly. He couldn't help his

children now, and Magda had probably killed herself as well. Here was his chance to live, and get away. He took the chance.

"Mein Führer, wait!" He shouted as he tried to catch up. He finally caught them rounding another corner.

Darkness hounded the hallway, of the stairs and out of the back of the bunker. There was a car, with no chauffeur, that they took to the air field , and the waiting plane

All three of them climbed in the plane, then cuddled up with the blankets. It seemed cold for April, chillingly cold.

Chapter 8

Once in the air, bullets whizzed past them in a fury. Joseph Goebbels was deep in thought about his dead wife and children. He knew they would assume him dead when they found the rest of his family killed by poison-how could they not?

The plane came to a quick landing strip in the town of Tonder, Denmark. They eventually made their way to Reus, a town south of Barcelona where the tyrant Franco gave them aid to the Canary Islands.

From there a monk who lived on the islands signed phony papers to get them to Mar Del Plata, Argentina- their final stop.

When they were destined at every stop to meet a Father or a Monk, it was not surprising to hear Eva wishing them *'Guten Morgen, mein Vater. Ich gelungen!'* (Good Morning, my Father. I succeeded!).

For at every stop they made, there happened to be a Catholic church.

Chapter 9

Eva sat silently as the plane engines roared. So much had happened already in her 33 years. She had been born to Fritz and Fanny Braun, highly respected middle-class citizens of pre-World War I, Munich. When she was born she already had a three-year-old sister, she would have another sister in three years.

Her father, Fritz, had wanted a boy. But when Eva was born, he got over his disappointment. The fact that he would have no son to carry on the family name would have to wait, for by the time her younger sister, Gretl had been born, he was in the German army.

On June 28,1914, when Gavrilo Princip, an Austro-Hungarian student, shot and killed Archduke Franz Ferdinand of Austria and his wife in the Bosnian capital of Sarajevo, Franz Braun immediately recognized the seriousness of the assassination. He was already aware of the antagonism between Austria-Hungary and Serbia, caused by the territorial demands of Serbia, and new while the assassin was of Austrian-Hungary nationality, he was a

Serbian by birth.

Franz Braun was not surprised when Austria-Hungary declared war on Serbia on July 28, an action that led to World War I, and eventually set the stage for Adolf Hitler's political career.

Eva was far too young to understand where her father had gone. She became so quiet that her mother had finally called the doctor, convinced she was ill. The old doctor couldn't find anything wrong with the child, and that she would return to her active self.

He was right. It was good that she returned to her old self, for she was badly needed at home. Her mother, Fanny, was having a hard time feeding her children.

She remembered one winter when they all lived on turnips. Meat, potatoes and butter had been in short supply and only available on the black market, and her mother didn't have the money to buy them. One thing she did was make army uniforms, and took in lodgers, anything to keep her small family warm and feed.

It had been estimated that three quarters of a million Germans died that winter from hunger; Fanny wasn't going to let that happen to her family.

Eva was six years old with her father eventually came home from the war. Inflation had wiped out the Braun's savings, as it had most of Germany.

Government bonds were not worth the paper they were printed on.

Though Fritz had resumed his teaching career, his salary was not enough to support his family in prewar comfort. Deprived of their sense of security, the Braun family felt betrayed by the government and deeply resented the triumphant allies at Versailles.

It was this economic breakdown and bitterness that gave birth to the numerous political parties that jockeyed for powerful position.

One of these was the Nation Socialist German Workers' Party (NSDAP), led by Adolf Hitler. Fritz Braun had refused to have anything to do with the Nazi organization, whose leader he considered to be a jack of all trades, who wanted to change the world.

In 1925, when Eva was 13 years old, her father inherited a modest sum of money from a distant aunt, and the family fortunes immediately took an upswing.

They moved into a larger apartment, closer to Luitpold Park. The family was also closer to Englischer Garten, which had a lake, horseback riding and several playgrounds.

Eva followed in her mother's footsteps, and soon became an excellent swimmer and ice skater. In winter she learned to ski the mountains south of Munich, where her family often went on long weekends. Fanny wanted more for her girls, and was concerned with Eva's formal education.

"She will only learn as long as she is amused," Fanny said to Fritz.

Actually, even attitude was influenced by the times she was living in. She often thought, *best to live today, because tomorrow may never come.*

Why study the music of Richard Wagner, when American jazz was better for dancing? By the time she was 15, Eva had the education expected of a girl her age, but did not explore the world of the classics.

All she wanted was to have a good time. Eva's strict upbringing and her Catholic background did have some effect on her. She was offered a cigarette and refused to smoke it. Then one evening, almost a year later, she was dared to smoke by a bunch of girlfriends.

It made her sick. She stuck to it and continued to smoke, despite Hitler's disapproval.

At 15, Eva became interested in boys, a fact that did not go over well with her father. She would occasionally bring a boy to the Braun apartment, after her mother would check out his reputation. But her father! Sometimes she would remember, he wouldn't even answer her when she would ask to go to the movies.

61

Her mother and father made a decision, Eva would attend convent school. She was determined that her girls would rise to a life above hers. A convent school education was the tool for learning social graces. All of this could be for Eva, if she were guided in her early years.

She was sent to the town of Simbach, 60 miles east of Munich, to a Catholic order set up by a group of English sisters, at the age of 16.

Eva later thought it was a strange coincidence that Simbach was directly across the Inn River from the Austrian town of Braunau, home of Adolf Hitler.

She found the life at the convent school hard, not to her liking at all. She endured the disciplined life without a fight. Eva found however, she did like one aspect of school, and that was acting.

Eva had always been intrigued by acting; although she never got to be the star, she would put all her vigor into school pageants.

She also was an excellent dancer, but found little opportunity to showcase her talents. She remembered that once she had been putting on a recital in her room for the other girls, and was caught.

"Around I go and where I stop, nobody knows!" Eva sang out during her recital.

"What is this?" Sr. Mary Beth demanded.

"I was dancing, to show the girls were I have learned, sister." Eva looked down at her feet.

"I will talk to the mother superior about this right away, I am sure you girls will be put on restrictions for this!" Sr. Mary Beth screamed.

"No!" Eva pleaded, "please sister, I asked them to watch me, because I have a new dance. It is my fault, punish me."

Eva endeared herself to the other girls because of this. She was beginning to find life unbearable at school, and made a promise to herself that all would change, if she ever got the chance.

One thing stood in her way, her father, Fritz Braun. When she returned home a year early from school, he became a monster about her following the rules of 'his castle'. He would make sure that she was home in bed by 10 o'clock, even shutting off electricity to her room by that time. She was very determined however, taking a flashlight with her to read under the covers.

Fritz was determined to break her. Or so he thought. Instead, it made Eva all the more determined to find excitement in her life outside the Braun apartment.

. . . .

It was the lack of money in the Braun circle that finally gave Eva excuse she needed to get away from the family. Although they had the inheritance and Fritz was not a full board professor, he didn't have money to give Eva for spending.

At first, Fritz thought *no* to Eva's getting a job, but later reconsidered. He had read about the depression in the United States, and new if history repeated itself, and surely it would, that Germany would feel its effects about a year later. He knew it would be good for Eva to bring in some money.

The was the last thing Eva thought about, she would use the money to buy clothes, jewelry, cosmetics and other personal items. Father could concentrate on her outlook in life, she would concentrate on her physical appearance. She had noticed her sister, Ilse, was using cosmetics now.

Since Ilse worked at a doctor's office, she said it was of vital importance to look her best.

Eva thought she was becoming plump, so she began to watch her weight. She began to buy clothes that were of the latest fashion. She also began to explore the world of cosmetics, which were a big help when she started job-hunting, especially if she noticed they were male employers. She knew that while it was fine for German girls to be plump, she wanted to be slim, but she knew her father would not have it. She faked having a nervous stomach, and faked it for so long that her mother had sent her to the doctor.

Eva told the doctor the truth.

"Oh Dr.," Eva began, "please won't you help me? My father

things I am being silly, but you will help me, won't you?"

"Yes Eva," the doctor said, "I will help you. As long as you don't start looking like a skeleton, I will be behind you."

"Oh danke! Danke shein!"

It took a few months, but it was finally starting to take effect, Eva was changing from a plump German girl into a fashionable young woman.

A girl who lived down the street teased Eva about her cosmetics once and was rebuffed by Eva.

"If a few pfennigs of cosmetics gets me what I want, then it is money well spent."

Another one of Eva's friends, Klara Oster, worked at the Park Hotel in Düsseldorf. During one afternoon together in the English gartens, Eva began to get a more sophisticated view of life.

"You see, Eva," Klara began to explain, "my earrings, yes those are real diamonds, and this bracelet, came from the gentleman I'm at my job."

"Vhy is that, Klara? Are you an excellent typist?" Eva innocently asked. Klara let out a huge laugh.

"Yes," Klara explained, "I am an excellent typist, but that is not vhy they give me gifts. There are 100 excellent typists in Düsseldorf, they give me gifts because I am nice to them. I go to dinner with them vhen they are lonely, and laugh at their jokes and keep them in good humor as much as possible."

Eva's face turned red.

"Do not get the wrong idea, Eva. I do not go that far."

Eva had been thinking about this when she was was with her sister, Ilse, later.

"I do not believe that men would give Klara such gifts just for being nice to them."

That is a dangerous game she is playing, but also very effective." Ilse said.

This was one lesson Eva would remember for the rest of her life.

Eva answered an ad concerning a position at a photography

shop. The owner was a short, heavy-set Bavarian named Heinrich Hoffman, a distinguished man who loved his drinking and women equally.

Hoffman was a very talented artist, who had studied under his father and uncle. He had moved around a bit, but soon settled in Munich and found himself a wealthy man. Hoffman was a confident man, who thought the hundred dollars he offered to provide a picture of the radical Hitler to an American agency in 1922 would be just another easy assignment. Hoffman, who had joined the Nazi party two years earlier, approved of the party's platform.

But he did not know Hitler. He discovered that he had a fetish about having his picture taken. He believed it was important to his hypnotic quality over people that they had never seen a picture of him.

So, Hoffman's pleas were ignored, and he didn't get the photograph. However, he did become friends with Hitler over the next two years, and that was a beginning.

Hitler spent many hours relaxing at the Hoffman house. It wasn't until 1924, when Hitler was released from the prison in Landsberg, that Hoffman was finally allowed to take his picture.

It was then that Hoffman became known as "Hitler's photographer," a title that was to bring him worldwide fame and wealth.

When Eva came into his shop in 1929, Hoffman was pleased by her appearance and youthfulness, both were good for business. He hired her to do work as a clerk, and to help them in the darkroom. Photography was to remain a lifelong past time of Eva's.

During this time, Hoffman taught her about politics, and the struggle that was in progress between Bavaria and Germany for control of the government. She noticed Hoffman being attentive to certain customers. She thought it was because they were wealthy, but in reality it was because they were associates of Hitler.

The names Rosenberg, Hess, Bormann, Himmler and Goebbles

meant nothing to her. Politics were not her interest in 1929.

Hoffman was keenly aware of his friendship with Hitler, and plotted his movement with him very carefully. He knew that Hitler was trying to maneuver his party into power, and if he did, Hoffman wanted to be at his side.

Therefore, every picture he took of Hitler had to be perfect. He would travel across Germany at a moments notice if Hitler requested it.

There was one other secret duty he had, and it was to keep a list of women, attractive women, to keep Hitler happy if he was lonely or bored.

There was a time when this duty was not necessary, when Geli Raubal, Hitler's niece, had moved into Hitler's apartment. Hoffman was surprised when Hitler then showed interest in the girl was on the ladder when he came into the shop. Eva was up getting a box of film when Hitler noticed her.

"Come down here Eva, I have an errand for you." She looked back, and saw Hitler.

She smiled.

Eva came down the ladder when Hoffman handed her down leberkaes and beer. Hoffman knew that Hitler wouldn't talk to the girl who was just a clerk unless he had good reason to do so. This getting together for something to eat gave him the perfect excuse to talk with the girl.

Hoffman introduced them, then later asked her what she thought of him.

"Herr Hoffman, I thought he was a friend of yours, that is why I was nice to him."

He was stunned. This girl had no idea who Hitler was. Hoffman was disappointed that anyone in Munich, or Bavaria could not know Hitler was. Hoffman grumbled as he walked away.

Eva could not understand why Hoffman was upset with her. She did remember his eyes, however. Not because they were blue, but because of their hypnotic quality. She was still thinking about his eyes that evening when she walked into dinner with her family and asked,

"Who is Adolf Hitler?"

That was the wrong question to ask in the Braun household.

"Adolf Hitler? My Got in Himmel! He is a fanatic. Do you hear me? A fanatic who thinks he can change the world by waving his hands. I am opposed to his political platform, they tried to get me to join the Nazi party, can you believe it, *me* a Nazi! I will not have it, by Got!" Fritz Braun went on and on ranting and raving about the Nazi party.

There was also a personal reason for Fritz disliking Hitler. He had been up for promotion until they found out he was not a member of the Nazi party, then promoted past him. Fritz had always disliked politics, but this was truly disgusting.

So when Eva brought up his name that evening, Fritz was furious. Poor Eva! She realized that his name had made her father so mad, so she changed the subject. Only now it had whet her appetite for knowledge about this man who wore the little mustache.

She spent the next day rummaging through Hoffmans vast collections of Hitler photographs. Some of the pictures fascinated Eva.

Here were pictures of Hitler at the opera with famous actresses. Eva had revised her opinion of Hitler.

He was a celebrity. Eva was eager for this man to come back into her life.

It was during this time that Hitler became very busy, and his visits to Hoffman's studio became rare. His speeches started to be heard all over Germany now, and the owners of German heavy industry were impressed by the way Adolf Hitler had riled up the enemies, and promised to back him financially if he would agree to cooperate.

In 1929, Hitler needed the money badly enough to agree to liaise . He had thought once he was in power he would be powerful and could dismiss them.

Eva was sad during this time. She had seen very little of him, although she had found out about his age, 40 years to her 17, and it made him seem like he was an old man. She wanted him even more. It was shortly after Hitler's signing of the Young Plan that he made an entrance back into Eva's life.

"Is Herr Hoffman in the back?" Hitler asked.
Young Eva looked up into his eyes. She was striking! She made her way back and brought Hitler with her.

After a time talking in the back, Hitler and Hoffman came to the front, Hitler made a bow, then left.

"I would like it very much if you would come to my house tonight. Hitler is stopping by and he asked me to bring you." Hoffman requested.

"I would be honored, Herr Hoffman." Eva felt her insides turn to jelly, just think, a night with Adolf Hitler!

That night at Hoffman's house they spent an evening talking art and photography, and Eva learned a valuable lesson. If she were going to attract the likes of Hitler, she would have to cater to his likes and dislikes.

"Herr Hitler," Eva began, "I was very impressed

74

with the file of photographs hair Hoffman has in his studio. I was especially impressed by the actresses and the other people of great importance seemed to be hanging on to you."

Eva lowered her eyes. Hitler showed signs of delight.

"Herr Hitler," Eva began, "one wonders why you have not chosen a bride, it looks like you could take your pick."

"But my dear," Hitler said, "my bride is Germany."

Eva didn't know what he meant by that, but Hoffman knew it was his way of saying that his country took the place of a bride in his heart

But what Hoffman and many others didn't know about Hitler was there was someone who took a special place in his heart already, Geli Raubal, his niece, who was living at his Prinzregentenstrasse apartment.

Eva knew nothing about Geli Raubal. In fact, by the way Hitler had blushed when Hoffman had begun telling one of his vulgar stories when Eva was in the room, Eva would have thought you were crazy to suggest that he had such a young mistress.

Hitler had thought women should not listen to stories like this in public, private was another matter.

Hoffman was told to arranged another meeting with Eva, and Hoffman told Julian Schaub was one person who knew the affair between Hitler and the infamous Geli Raubal. Geli also found out about Eva.

Hitler's apartment was divided into two wings: one for him, and the other for Geli. In reality, she stayed closer to his bedroom, luxuriously decorated with antiques from Austria.

Geli's mother slept in a room across from her daughters anteroom, and both shared a bathroom. Fraü Annie Winter and her husband managed the servants while Geli's mother was in charge of the whole household.

Geli was 22 years old; she had met him when her mother joined him at his mountain retreat, Haus Wachenfeld. Hitler made sure that she moved with her mother to Munich to be near him. He would have loved it if she would have stayed at the mountain retreat, but he was keenly aware of his image. Hitler didn't want the public to think he had time to waste on private matters of the heart.

In 1931 it was common knowledge in Munich that Hitler and Geli were having an affair, and that it had the unpleasant suggestion of incest. Hitler made no attempt to hide his feelings for Geli, often appearing with her on his arm in public.

Contrary to popular beliefs, Geli seemed agreeable to the affair as Hitler. She was a sexually promiscuous girl who toyed with many men, if she was sure her uncle would not find out. Geli loved her life with Adolf, he gave her money to buy clothes, cosmetics, anything her heart desired. She desired to bask in the glow of his celebrity. She would do anything, sexually and otherwise, to keep his attention.

Wilhelm Stocker, who was a former SA officer, told about how when Hitler was away at a convention or otherwise, she would have her way with other men. And of course, to buy his silence, she would perform her sexual acts on him.

"You know how I am often stuck here with Adolf," Geli began, "he does things that I cannot even bring myself to tell you. It is sickening."

"Vhy do you allow him to do them? Vhy do you not stop him?" Stocker would ask. "Vhat exactly does he do to you?"

Geli allowed her eyes to travel around the room, then landed square on Stocker's eyes.

"I would do anything he asked, but I hate vhen he makes me perform." Geli said.

"Perform?"

"Ja, he makes me perform the act."

"The act?" Stocker asked, "vhat is 'the act?' Come, Geli- you must tell me!"

"He makes me urinate and defecate standing over his face." Geli said.

"My Gott! Geli, you must not do this anymore."

"I do not want to lose him to some other girl who would do vhat he needs." Geli said through her tears. "I vill do vhatever he vants, I am his puppet."

Geli was willing to do what she had to, to remain Hitler's favorite.

In 1931, it seems that she was no longer Hitler's favorite, there was another woman. The other woman was Eva Braun. He treated them completely different. The blonde Geli he would take on his arm to the openings of plays, and other such things.

Eva would be treated as though she were a secret to the world. He would meet her at Hoffman's house, spend the evening there, then have his chauffeur dropped her off at her parents apartment to meet later and spend the rest of the evening alone with her.

As Hitler's popularity grew in 1931, Geli and Eva fought even harder to win his attention. Though they never saw each other, they knew about the others existence.

Once, when Hoffman took Eva to Fashing (the Munich carnival) in 1931, they entered the festival beer tents and saw Hitler and Geli sitting at one of the tables. Not wanting the girls to meet, Hoffman took Eva to a table at the far end of the tent.

Having fun with the situation, Hoffman started introducing Eva

79

as 'my niece', and allusion to the Hitler-Geli affair.

Later, when Geli found out about it, she was furious.

"How dare she!"Geli screamed, "I will not be put in the same class as that monkey faced girl."

Geli had found out the girl had been Eva Braun.

Although Hitler managed to keep his budding romance secret, Geli was painfully more aware of it in 1931.

Hitler made more and more trips to Hoffman's house, forcing Geli to go to parties alone. When Hitler found out about it he grew furious. But since they always kissed and made up afterward, nobody took it seriously.

It was serious. Geli had made up her mind that Hitler was not going to make her a fool by playing around with Eva. She had found a letter in Hitler's pocket, a letter from Eva.

"I do not want that baboon writing letters to you, do you hear me? No more!" Geli screamed at him.

"And I can help it if the girl is in love with me? Vhat do I have to do about it?" Adolf would counter.

Less than a month later, Hitler had begun a campaign to the north of Germany, with Hoffman going along to take some pictures. Hoffman was helping Hitler to pack and didn't pay much attention to their fight, but thought it was strange when he heard Hitler yell to the girl,

"Shut up!' Hitler came out of the room, and motioned that he was ready to go. When they were loading up their bag in the Mercedes, a red-faced Geli appeared in the window, and Hitler turned red and said to her,

"For the last time, Geli, NO!"

Off they went, when Hoffman look back he saw that Geli had been crying. Later when Geli went to the Munich Playhouse with Frau Schaub, she was lost to the world.

Geli would start crying for no apparent reason. During intermission,Geli bought a chocolate bar and drink, and seemed to be getting along better. On the way home,Geli asked Frau Schaub what her plans were, since she knew she would be joining Hitler in a few days to be with her husband.

"I have no plans," Frau Schaub said, "I will be in my apartment if you get lonely."

Those were the last words spoken to Geli, for the next morning Fraü Winter called Fraü Schaub and asked if Geli had spent the night with her, that she was late coming down for her morning tea. Then a call was put into her mother, who was vacationing at the Obersalzberg.

Nothing. Then she notified her husband and together they broke down Geli's door.

She was dead. Shot through the heart, with the pistol in her hand. The letters to Adolf Hitler written by Eva Braun were on the dresser.

Adolf had to be notified immediately.
Adolf raced home, but there was nothing he could do. He turned into himself for a short time, then suddenly came out, with Eva Braun at his side.

What a glorious time for Eva! She had her man to herself. Never again would she let another woman come between her and her Adolf.

Chapter 10

Middle of October, 1945

Adolf sat back, he could hear the crickets tonight. They did not bother him. He sat, thinking of the possibilities before him. Goebbels knocked lightly on the door.

"Heir Hitler," he began, "it is late, but perhaps you could not sleep with all that it has happened."

Adolf answered with a wave of his hand. It was true, so much had happened.

Poor Eva. It was during the time Hitler had managed to plan for their escape that Eva had toppled down the winding stairway in the submarine and broken her arm.

Her leg had been scraped up pretty badly, but escape Germany they did. All in all, not bad. As far as that U-boat ride they took to Argentina. The jungle outside was scorching. Too hot for Adolf's taste.

It was sticky as well, and those damn bugs! He sat there thinking and shoved a hand under his nightshirt to scratch one of a multitude of mosquito bites.

It was October in Argentina, and not a very forgiving one. Goebbels walked over to pour himself a drink of water. He wished it could have been something else, schnapps, perhaps.

Could the Almighty Führer ever know what it was like to see his own children die? And what about his wife? He wondered if Hitler ever had a thought for anyone else. Goebbels wanted to die.

His insides were churning with hatred for this man who so callously let him put his own family to die by poison. All because he said there was only room for one aboard the U-boat. He had bought it. He had seen with his own eyes how there was room enough for his whole family. Hold on- it was wrong to think like that. Yes, wrong.

He tried again to make conversation.

"What do you think, mein Führer, about what was brought up yesterday by the U-boat commander? That you need to make a new start somewhere?"

Adolf had been thinking of exactly the same thing.

"Eva needs her sleep. Ve should go elsewhere."

They quietly walked out of the room onto the veranda. There was a breeze, but still it was warm it was an extremely humid night in Argentina. The breeze made the palm trees wave with the sound of the ocean faraway.

It was one of Juan Perone's hideouts, secure, nestled in the hills surrounded by his guards. Perone had made it his business to provide the hideouts needed by so many Nazi escapees. They had been wanted by the world, but so what? Juan Perón made it legal for the Nazis to be in his country.

Adolf felt a friendship with Perón, surely a friendship he could count on in his time of need.

Adolf leaned over the balcony.

"I was thinking about the same thing when you came in," he continued, "I was thinking about the plastic surgery, for all of us. Then I was thinking 'North'." He pointed.

"Passports and identification will not be a worry for us, as you know. Because here we have friends in the government, high

86

friends. Ve Vill continue our way north and continue our work."

Adolf stopped for a moment. His face contorted. He was thinking about the Russians, and how that bastard Stalin had betrayed him.

"Oh, vhat a terrible loss we suffered to have the Russians come vhen they did," Adolf said, "Dr. Mengele had been doing so much with his research, and so many of the Jewish maggots had been cleaned off the earth. So much for the Aryan race."

But the Russians did come. They came at a time when it would do Hitler the most harm. He was a feeble old man. His hands were shaking so badly that he kept them hidden in his pockets most of the time.

Last days of war were hell for Adolf Hitler. At least he had Eva. He also had the knowledge that there were factions out there that believed in him still. He sat with Eva, stroking her blonde hair with his hands shaking tremendously.

"My Eva." He said quietly, "my poor Eva."

His words woke her from sleep.

"Adolf," she began, "vhat are you doing here? It's dark, you should be asleep."

"I vanted to be here in case you woke up, lepshen." His voice cracked and it was weak. "I vanted to be here."

Eva felt more like her old self. The cast on her arm hurt, and she wasn't so sure about her legs, they were scratched and bruised, but she felt better than she had in days. She was sure now was as good a time as any to tell the news to Adolf.

"Shatz," she began, "I vant to tell you something, and I do not know how to do it, so I vill just do it…" She began rubbing his hands with her good hand,

"Adolf, I am with child."

The silence in the room was deafening. Even knew she had just dropped a bomb that was his big as any they have heard at the bunker. Adolf, who had been sitting there letting her rub his hands, suddenly threw his hands in the air and started shouting.

"My Gott in Himmel! Eva, are you sure?"

Eva wasn't sure if he was happy or distraught. She very quietly said, "I am sure I am pregnant." She paused then went on.

88

"Vould you allow me to have this baby? You vill not take it from me, vill you?" Eva started crying softly at first then it became uncontrollable.

Adolf then said, "I must know Eva, is it mine?"

It was obvious to Eva that he must be thinking of Geli, and all her men. She nodded her head.

"Then I must be happy, no? I must be." He walked to the end of the room decorated so lavishly, then walked back to Eva.

"Eva," Adolf shouted, "then I am happy, my Schatz!"

Chapter 11

Part II

Adam Levy was leaving the synagogue that afternoon. He had been talking to the Rabbi about what he had told them at the funeral. It was still hard to believe, but it was slowly starting to make sense. It had been so many years since his father had stopped looking for Adolf Hitler.

Only now it was his search, Adam Levy's search, to find the infamous Führer. Adam knew from his father's journals that he had left off somewhere in Argentina. It kind of made sense when Adam learned what kind of man Agmon was, no wonder he always seemed like he was in his own world, like part of him died.

No wonder he seemed to be away, if he had only told us what he had on his mind. If only he shared his grief with us!

Agmon had believed that Hitler had faked his own suicide and had lived in South America. Only South America did not give away it's clues. Adam only believed part of that story, that Hitler *was* alive, some years ago, but that he was probably long ago dead. Adam Levy was *not* a Nazi hunter, but since his father had been one, he now felt that it was the only thing to give Agmon some peace, to put to rest the Nazi regime that had plagued him all his life.

Agmon had escaped the horror of the concentration camps when he was a very small boy. He had been born in Austria, and remembered the horror of the escape to Switzerland, and then the underground passageways to a place where you get passage to America.

His whole family, father, mother and little sister Sara, had all been caught and killed in concentration camps. This time he swore he would never forget, and became a Nazi war hunter, going to south America when ever there was evidence of the men and women of the Nazi party.

Adam knew about this time from reading his journals and it made him angrier than ever when he read about his grandparents and aunt dying the way they did. But still, it was now the time

passed 2005, what could possibly be going on now? He knew he

had to talk about this with Gretchen.

"Gretch," Adam started, "we need to talk."

"What about?" Gretchen turned her head to Adam.

"Dad."

"I'm glad you started this." Gretchen said, "because I have

found out a few things I needed to talk to you about, too."

Chapter 12

Adam and Gretchen Levy were a study in opposites.

Adam was a tall young man, with dark hair that curled at

the ends. He had blue eyes, just like his mother's, but in

every other way looked like his father.

Gretchen had blonde, super straight hair that at it's ends

was to her tailbone. They were both slender built, but Gretchen

looked like their mother.

Adam liked to surf, and did so daily, while Gretchen was

happiest reading a book on the shore. Although they were both

in school, with Gretchen getting ready to join Adam at the

university, neither one of them had seriously dated a person of

the opposite sex.

They had always had a special bond as brother and sister.

Now that they were alone in the world they felt as though they

wanted to make it tighter still.

Gretchen started, "I found out the most amazing things about

dad."

"What did you find out, because I have read his journals and there's some stuff I want to share with you, some really morbid stuff."

"I have to say, that some things were buried deep in the Internet-but I did some digging and I found out that there are Nazi organizations still in operation today." Gretchen said. "And I'm not talking about Nazi Germany, I'm talking Nazi Norway, Denmark and all over South America."

"You have got to be kidding me," Adam said, "Norway and Denmark? I've heard about South America from history class, but I never knew that it was in Norway and Denmark!"

"And I'm not talking about Nazis in the dark, they are right out in the open, where everyone can see them." Gretchen exclaimed.

"I don't think that dad even knew about the new Nazis, but I don't think since he stopped chasing Nazis, since mom died, that he even cared." Adam said.

"I've read a lot of material, how Nazi hunters like Simon Wiesenthal chased Nazis his whole life. But there seems to be a gap, since 2005 when Wiesenthal passed away no one seems to care about chasing Nazis anymore." Gretchen said.

"Maybe that's because there all dead." Adam shrugged his shoulders.

"Hardly." Gretchen scoffed, "here, look at these- they are pictures of the new Nazi generals. Look closely, these are young guys. Some of them don't even look like they're past their 20s!"

"I'll be damned." Adam admitted, "you're right."

"See how it says what country there in under their pictures. It looks like we have a few living right here in the US." Gretchen said.

"My God," Adam said, "there are even a few in Canada!"

"So do you think they're all dead anymore?" Gretchen asked.

"Not if the Internet is to be believed." Adam said.

"Now," Gretchen said, "what did you have to tell me?"

Adam shared with her the contents of their fathers journals. When he finished, Gretchen had started to tear up.

"Those bastards!" Gretchen said, "I believe you, I god damned believe you!"

They both loved their father profoundly, but since finding out about him through his journals, and what they were able to dig up on the Internet, that love turned into a deep respect.

Chapter 13

Adam and Gretchen Levy's search brought them to Argentina. The government had always been so welcoming to Nazis trying to get away, so they weren't even sure what help the government would be.

Agmon's journals had mentioned the name of a doctor who specialized in plastic surgery who had been killed in 1946 by unusual means. They were going to find out more about the doctor.

It seemed that Dr. Morres had a living daughter. The police have not questioned her at the time because she was a little girl. Agustina, his daughter, had grown and married and was left a widow with a rather large fortune. She was in her early 70s, and had begun to live in altogether sheltered life.

Her compound was vast and beautiful. Agustina had taken up floral architecture, and was busy tending to her vibrant colored flowers. Adam and Gretchen finally found her compound on the edge of Buenos Aires. They had finally made their way to the top of the hill then knocked on her door.

A small elderly woman answered the door, and you could tell by her dress, a maid.

"Buenos dias, madam. My name is Adam Levy and this is my sister, Gretchen. Is Agustina here?"

The old lady shrugged her shoulders and without saying a word took Adam and Gretchen through the hallway to the library. The old lady said something in Spanish and left them alone in the library.

"Did she understand you, Adam?"

"I don't know if she understood English well enough to know we were here to see Agustina. But after all the work we put into finding her it was remarkably easy to see her, I mean I thought would run into bodyguards guarding her, but she just showed us in."

"Weird, huh?" Gretchen said.

Just then the huge double doors opened and in walked

98

Agustina. She was dressed in a blue and gold caftan. It was easy to see that her perfectly coiffed hair was not her own, as the wig sat askew on her head. With her age came cataracts as you could tell when she did not look directly at you when she spoke.

"Buenos dias, Agustina. I'm Adam and this is my sister Gretchen. Remember we called you about…"

"Hallo is more appropriate this far into the country. German is my native tongue, Spanish is what the low landers use." Agustina said curtly.

"Oh, I apologize for that. But your English is very good." Adam said.

"I hardly ever use English. German, as I said, is the tongue I use." Agustina made her way to the long couch, and said, "why are you here?"

"As my brother has already told you on the phone, we are looking into the death of your father." Gretchen said.

"Yes I know that, but what I want to know is why? The police never even asked me about what I knew. And I knew plenty, but

99

as I said they never asked."Agustina said.

"We'll were not from this country, I guess you can tell because we speak English. What we're looking for is information on his unusual death." Adam said.

"Yes, I understand that. But as I will say only one more time is 'why?'" Agustina was getting angrier now, as she started scratching the arm rest.

"Well that's kind of a long story." Gretchen said.

"I have nothing but time. So please, tell me your story."Agustina said.

"Our story is this," Adam began, "it is because of our father. He is, or rather was, a Nazi hunter. This was many years ago, before we were even born. He left us journals tracking Adolf Hitler. His journal also mentioned your father and the tragic way he died. Our father is dead now, and it is out of respect for our father that we are here. Can you help us?"

Agustina started to tremble. Then she started to gently shake all over. A tear came out of her eye,and then she began to say,

"I can hardly believe my ears, after all these years, after all these years."

"Can you remember?" Gretchen asked.

"I may look old to you, child-but I can remember what I have been wanting to say for years." Agustina said.

"Then please," Adam said, "tell us what you know."

"It was 1946 and I myself was a child. My father was a great plastic surgeon. People used to come from all over the world so they could have use of his hands." Agustina began, "the Germans started coming here, the Nazis. Juan Peron was courting them, telling them that they were welcome in our country. Did you know that Juan Peron also courted Jewish people? My father was Jewish."

"No, we had no idea." Adam said.

"He was a Jew. Juan Peron had people coming into our country with no regard to what would happen when he did. Can you imagine? 1946 with Nazis and Jews in the same country? Peron only cared about the money the Nazis would bring. It was if he didn't care about what would happen to the Jewish people."Agustina said with a glint in her eye. "So my father got a call from somebody high up in the government who said that he was to perform plastic surgery on a group of people no questions asked. He changed their noses, their eyes slightly just enough so you wouldn't be able to tell who they were. It was the last day, the day when he had dealt with any swelling when it happened."

Adam put his hand on her arm, and she reciprocated by padding his hand.

"I was in his office when this group of people came in. Yes, he did a good job. You really could not tell who they were, but I knew. For the lady repeatedly called the man who was in charge, 'Schatzi' and then Adolf. And he called her, 'Eva'. I do not know who everyone was, but I do know it was Adolf Hitler and his wife Eva." Agustina said.

Adam and Gretchen looked at each other with great excitement in their eyes. Adam said,

"Are you sure?"

"As sure as my name is Agustina."

Chapter 14

Agustina turned and started walking for the huge double doors. She knew every inch of her house by now, and knew where everything was placed. Adam and Gretchen followed behind, and they took their breath away when they went through the facing double doors and suddenly they were in a garden in the middle of the compound.

Adam took a deep breath, and looked at the open and airy mansion, with palm trees growing from the middle of the foyer all the way down to the garden.

Agustina closed her eyes and starting to cough. She picked up her gardening shears and started to cut off the dead heads off the Jasmine bushes which gave off the most agreeable fragrance. How she knew the difference between the two they never knew.

Gretchen started the next round of questions.

"Agustina," she said, "please. Won't you continue?"

"Ja. I will continue. Is it not strange how the past lives on in the future?"

"It is very strange, Miss Agustina. If I didn't read my father's journals, I would've never found out about your father and the way he died. My father's journals didn't specify how your father died-could you tell us?" Adam said.

"On the last day, when they murdered my father, they put a burlap bag over his head. I was in the very room when my father was taken. But I do not know if they even saw me. I was in the corner counting my money, behind the desk, for my father was teaching me to count. The woman, Eva, told the man, Adolf to hurry. She said they had to pick up their son from the nanny, who she said, was also one that had to die that day. They pulled my father's arms behind his back and tied them together with rope. There were five of them, all five had had work done to their faces." Agustina stopped.

She clipped one more head off the Jasmine and seemed to regain her strength.

"They pushed my father out of the room and into a waiting van. That was the last time I saw him alive. Five days later we heard from the police saying that they found a headless torso, but it seemed to be my father by the identification they found on him."Agustina turned towards Adam and Gretchen.

Her eyes started to glow, as if she could suddenly see them.

"They found his head two weeks after that.

There were things done to his head, wretched things. Satanic things."

"Oh?" Adam said. "Satanic things?"

"Ja."

"How could you tell?" Gretchen asked.

"His head was burned, and it had been severed cleanly, but burned nonetheless. There were markings carved into his forehead, pentagrams and swastikas. There was also an upside down cross carved into the back of his head. Doesn't that say Satanic to you? It did to me." Agustina said. "My father had been a wreck for about six weeks before he was missing, now we knew why. His surgical assistant was also found murdered, but that's another story."

"And the police never asked you about this? None of it?" Adam asked.

"Nein. None of it. My mother was always afraid that they would come after us, but they never did. I think, nein, I know, that they left the country."

"What makes you think they left the country?" Gretchen asked.

"Because the one tall, spindly man dropped a bundle of passports on the floor before me. Killing my father must have been the last thing to do before they left."Agustina said.

"My God." Gretchen looked like she would be sick.

"Are you okay Gretch? Do you need some water?" Adam said.

"I'll be fine. Adam, do you realize that dad was right? Do you realize Adolf Hitler is alive, or at least he was alive past 1946."

"Eva Braun- Hitler was alive, too. But bigger problem here is that Adolf Hitler had a son!" Adam exclaimed.

There was one other item that Agustina knew, though she didn't tell it to Adam and Gretchen, and that was that there was another man who had an appointment with her, another man who was looking for the man known to them as Hitler. Though she didn't know who that was, she knew she was frightened of him, frightened of the letters NKGB. Agustina had every right to be scared of this man.

Chapter 15

The snow came down sideways in Russia. Freidrich Nicolai was walking in the wall of snow that was up to his thighs, mumbling about how he hated winter. He secretly wished for the long summer evenings of the tropics, where he had been stationed for the last five years.

Nicolai was going to the Kremlin, to the offices of KNGB, the organization where he had worked all his life. The KNGB was the Soviet secret police whose name had changed so many times over the years.

Up until a year ago he had a wife, a beautiful wife, God rest her soul. He had nursed her through her cancer most faithfully, but it in the end the breast cancer overcame her and she died after she had been put under morphia and she finally found peace.

They had a son and a daughter, who were busy raising their own families when they found out about their mother's cancer. Since Freidrich and Alina were in the Cuba when the cancer started, and Freidrich jr. and Marie, their children, were still living in Russia they never had the chance to see their mother one more time. They were too busy with their own children to say goodbye to their own mother, and since Friedrich had never forgiven them, it was like living in Russia on his own.

That is why he still worked, to keep his mind busy and his body active. After all the years of being in Argentina, Cuba, and other places had made a grand impression on him. America had made the greatest impression on him. People in America were spoilt, and living in a fool's paradise.

I'm getting old, too old for the games they want me to play.

Although he was an old man now he knew he was a very valuable game piece for NKGB. He had been responsible for finding at least 75 Nazi's around the world who had been wanted for war crimes against Russia. He was a short, stocky man approaching his mid-80s, but the man did love his travel. This was the only practical way he knew to travel for free.

The time he had spent with his wife at the end had just about wiped out their savings, but he knew he could go back to the

NKGB and get another assignment, and escape the cold, wintry weather of Russia once again.

Nicolai trudged up the long stairs of the Kremlin. Wiping his boots along the way.

Nicolai walked into the offices passed a little girl of a secretary and into his bosses office. He loved the NKGB organization, but come on! His boss?!

A kid, more like it. Barely 40 years old and my boss to boot, blyad!

Nicolai made himself comfortable on an old chair in a corner of the office. It was an old decrepit office but had some items to remind you of who was the boss.

Pictures hung around the room of his boss shaking hands with important dignitaries, even the President of the United States. There was also a picture on his desk of him and his family. There were six of them.

Rather a large family, father, mother, two girls and two boys, carbon copies of their father.

"What is it you want me to do today, or should I say rather who is it you want me to find?" Nicolai asked, "is this another goose chase? Or perhaps you would want me to find the Führer?" Nicolai laughed out loud in his hearty Russian voice, but stopped when he realized his boss wasn't laughing back.

"What is it?" Nicolai anxiously asked.

"Friedrich," his boss, Vadim, started, "we have received word from our man down in Argentina that there has been a man and a woman nosing around asking questions about Hitler. It seems they uncovered some evidence that might be of some use to us. Evidence that went unnoticed, even by you."

Nicolai didn't like his tone. He always made sure that everything he researched was thorough, very thorough.

"What kind of evidence are you talking about? I researched every bit of information that came our way and nothing came of it." Nicolai demanded.

"It seems there was a boy really, and his sister nosing about near Buenos Aires. Their father was a Nazi hunter, they are half

112

Jewish, it seems. Perhaps you've heard of Agmon Levy?" Vadim replied.

Nicolai nodded his head. Agmon Levy, yes. They had crossed paths before. He curled his hands into fists.

"It seems," Vadim continued, "they turned up the daughter of a plastic surgeon who had been killed horribly some years ago. It sounds funny to me that he would be interested in this doctor if he wasn't looking for something else. So I ask myself, what would the son and daughter of Agmon Levy be doing in Argentina talking to the daughter of a man who had long since been dead? Don't you see? It just sounds funny." Vadim's face looked drawn.

Nicolai made a sour face. Following in the footsteps of Agmon Levy's children wasn't what he had in mind.

"Perhaps they were doing a favor for their father. Or maybe they went to Argentina for another reason." Nicolai expressed his opinion.

"No," Vadim persisted, "no, I have had them checked out. Agmon is dead. His wife died some time ago. All that is left is

Adam and Gretchen. Adam likes sports, but it is no longer soccer season. Even so, he would not have to go all the way to Argentina to catch a game. His sister, Gretchen, spends most of her time on the computer or reading books- so you see, there really is no reason for their turning up in Argentina." Vadim wrapped his fingers around a little Russian doll that was on his desk. Then he continued, "I would feel better about it if you went and checked it out yourself."

"Da." Nicolai mimicked back, "then I will go." He looked behind Vadim's desk and said, "Do you think they know?"

"Would you tell your children?" Vadim asked.

Nicolai shook his head. Then he said, "When I come back, you and me, will finally drink some of the vodka I gave you for your birthday, eh? I've noticed that bottle sitting there crying out my name."

Vadim looked concerned. He looked at Nicolai and his Russian laugh began. "Friedrich, you know I could drink you under the table." He reached for his stomach, "but now, well you know how

114

it is. The doctors say, 'no more' and I have to oblige. So is the way of ulcers."

Nicolai thought about it. His doctor had given him orders not to drink, but he still did.

"Do not worry," Nicolai said, "your secret is safe with me."

Nicolai gave his boss a punch to the stomach. He groaned.

'*Kiska!'* Nicolai thought. *Pussy!*

*

Nicolai fell into a deep sleep on the flight to Argentina. He could not understand how people could not sleep on planes, he slept as soundly as a baby. There was a small tapping on his shoulder,

"Excuse me, sir." The flight attendant said, "we will be landing in a few minutes, and I need to get everyone sitting upright."

Just as well, good time as any to go over the dossier for this mission. This woman, named Agustina, is in her 60's, she is

rich, too.

Nicolai continued to go over the paperwork. She was living in the hills overlooking the city in some sort of compound. He also went over the paperwork for her father, killed in 1946.

Yes, this is interesting.

How could he have overlooked the murder? It was just another of the hundreds of murders that occurred in the city per year, according to the police, but still. He thought he had gone over all points. This sudden team coming from Agmon concerned him deeply.

Agmon's children, what did they find out? This is their first time out, it seems, did they get lucky?

Nicolai traveled with his carry-on bag and nothing else. He went straight from the plane to the que of people waiting for a cab, then straight to the hotel. He sat back and his headache grew, as the driver made his way through the tangled web of rush hour traffic.

Once he checked into his room he went straight up to his room and collapsed on the bed. He wasn't getting any younger, the time change had wiped him out.

The room was dark when Nicolai woke up again. The room was spinning around him. He stumbled over to the nightstand and took his pills. He laid his head down on the pillow and in the room started to fill normal again. He hated those awful cortisone pills he had to take, but he took them anyway. The doctor had told him he had to take them for the rest of his life, but just the same, Nicolai fought it.

He looked at the alarm clock in his room, 7 o'clock. He did not know if it was seven in the morning or seven at night. He picked up the phone and call the front desk, it was evening. Good, there was still time to visit the doctor's daughter.

On the way up to her compound he put no thought into their being different parts of the city- one extremely poor, the other opulently rich.

He had known over the lessons of a lifetime that it would always be, so be it. There were houses if you could call

117

corrugated tin roofs and dirt floors, houses up and down the, slippery slopes. The children ran around them, looking dirty and skinny unsupervised, and there seemed to be no end to them. Chickens ran loose, and so did pigs. Once he saw a poor woman in her ratty mu mu rounding up the children, for what reason he didn't know.

Not far from these houses where the rich houses, made of stone and sparkling glass windows. All you could see was the occasional gardener working on the grounds. Manicured lawns or dirt floors, there didn't seem to be a middle-class. Yet here they were living side-by-side in the city that seem to have room them both.

Finally Nicolai arrived at her mansion. The time was 7:45 and Nicolai was sure that she had not gone to bed. He rang the doorbell. The small maid answered the door and said some words that sounded Spanish to him.

"Madam Morres, por favor?"

The hunched over maid showed him to the drawing room.

"Gracias." Nicolai said.

"Please do not use Spanish here!" Agustina snapped at him.

"Fine. What would you have me use?" Nicolai replied.

"German. Or English."

"Madam Morres," Nicolai tried again, "I am here because I want to know about your father's death."

"First the police want nothing to do with that case, and suddenly a troop of people, come onto my property wanting to know what happened that day in 1946. Odd, would you not say?" Agustina said with the same ferocity that she started this conversation.

"Yes, I know you recently gave an account to some very young people from America. I want to know what you told them." Nicolai said.

"I understood why they came here looking for information. But I am having trouble understanding why you came here wanting the same information."

It became obvious that Nicolai's manner was changing. He was changing from polite to anger with no space between them.

"Look here, Fraulein," Nicolai said with spittle starting to collect in the corners of his mouth, "I want that information, and I want it now. It is up to you how I am going to get it."

"Look here, I do not even know what your name is, but nobody comes into my house demanding anything of me! I think it is time for you to leave." Agustina said matching his anger.

Nicolai walked across the room to a table filled with vases filled with flowers and knocked a dry one to the ground. Then keeping control of his anger he tried again.

"Ms. Morres," he tensely put his words together, "I know about Adam and Gretchen. I know they were here. And I know you gave them information about your father's murder that happened in 1946. 1946, that is a long time ago. I would hate to have anything happen now because of something that happened way back then, what do you think?" Nicolai stepped behind Agustina and wrapped his fingers around her neck.

Agustina turned so she faced him. She had as much spirit as he had, perhaps more.

"Why don't you go ahead and do it? I can feel the strength in your fingers, all you have to do is squeeze. I do not have to do anything you say, I will die before I let a man tell me what to do."

Nicolai loosened his grip, and finally let his hands fall.

"Forgive me, Ms. Morres." Nicolai said with his voice visibly softened, "you are right. I was being horribly rude to you. Perhaps if I told you why I want to know, then may be you will see why you should tell me."

Agustina sat down. This was something that her father had taught her-never show your fear, never!

But that does not mean that she didn't feel the fear-oh, no! She was still feeling the freight leave her body when she sat.

"Tell me,"Agustina asked, "what is your name?"

"My name is Friedrich, Friedrich Nicolai. And it is of vital importance that you tell me what you told them. Their lives depend on it." Nicolai slammed his fist on the table, upsetting one of Agustina's vases, spilling water on the credenza.

"Why is what happened to my father so long ago, important to those children's futures?" Agustina said keeping an even beat in her voice.

"Because my country demands to know why they are hunting the particular murderer, who if I were to believe them would change history. You must tell me, who did you tell them murdered your father?" Nicolai picked up the vase, trying to re- place the Jasmine.

"And what country is that, Mr. Nicolai?"

"Why do you want to know, I think you can tell by my accent what country I come from." Nicolai now rubbed his hands, they hurt.

"Your accent is *not* a peasant's, I believe you come from the northwest of your country, am I correct?" Agustina said.

"I originated in a town which seem to be in the middle of nowhere. But as I grew, I moved to the north. I learned many things, proper pronunciation is important in my country." Nicolai said.

"As it is in mine."

"Russia is my homeland. I would do anything for the motherland, any thing!" Nicolai's nostrils flared.

"I have no doubt you would do things to me in order to get information. Do I look scared to you?" Agustina said as she straightened her back.

"See here, Ms. Morres, I am too old to go chasing ghosts that don't even exist anymore." Nicolai was exhausted. All he wanted to do was sleep.

Her diminutive maid scurried into the room to clean up the spilled water. Agustina stood and waved her hands as if sign language was enough for her to get her point across.

"No." Nicolai folded his arms across his sunken chest. "You do not look scared . But let me tell you one thing, if the man who killed your father is the man that I am seeking, these young people have put their lives in danger. Was the man who killed your father, Adolf Hitler?"

The name caused Agustina's knees to buckle. Nicolai reached

out and grabbed her before she could fall.

"It was him, was it not?"

"Yes. The man who killed my father was Adolf Hitler. Now you know. What will you do to save them?" Agustina turned away with a pained look. Then she smiled her perfect little smile. "I told Adam and Gretchen that Hitler killed my father, but I told them something that I fear even more-that Hitler and Eva had a child. A son."

"NE'T!" Nicolai gasped, he muttered in a disbelieving voice. "Do you tell me this truth to God's ears?"

"I will swear to God, as I am standing here today." She inhaled deeply through her nose, then slowly exhaled through her mouth.

"I *will* do what I can, you can be sure of that!" Nicolai's eyes were on the door as he ran out of her mansion. He knew it, he *knew* it. Adolf Hitler was alive, just as he had been telling his superiors for decades. His head was spinning now, but unlike before it wasn't his lack of pills that caused it, it was the truth of knowing that Hitler's child, a son, was in this world.

Chapter 16

Chills trickled over Nicolai's churning stomach as he thought about the things Agustina had told him. He had seen things that would turn an ordinary man's insides to liquid, but what she conveyed was disturbing, even to him.

Nicolai was going over the police records, and had found the doctors head and his leg severed clean off. The police had also found a crudely drawn upside down cross, a five pointed star, or pentagram, a few burned down candles and the word 'natas'. The report was written so long ago, Nicolai had the feeling that the policeman who wrote the report were superstitious.

The way they glossed over the murder, or maybe they were being quiet on purpose? It certainly had dawned on him the severity of the idea of Hitler's being alive would cause. Was the government hiding him? He could see a war breaking out over this kind of thing.

Nicolai's fatigue was not being helped by the continual change in time zones. He tried to make a pillow for his head with the old jacket he had brought along, the pillows they used on his flight were ridiculous. A few more punches made his jacket palatable for him to take a short nap. When he woke a few hours later they were just starting their descent to Oahu.

A rare and glorious gift, Honolulu was all the things Nicolai hated about Americans. It was a balmy 74° with gentle westerly wind, and while Nicolai was waiting in line to get his taxi he tried to remember that he didn't like this country.

He could smell the macadamia nuts the vendor on the corner was selling, along with the smells of birds of paradise, and hibiscus, and they were breathtaking. He also thought he could faintly smell a cooking sea bass coming from the nearby hotels restaurant. When he got to his hotel his room overlooks the ocean, and he stood there for nearly 3 minutes before his hatred had turned to admiration.

Ah! This is what I call life.

Now was time to find Adam and Gretchen Levy. He picked up his address book and slowly wandered down to the restaurant to have the sea bass underneath some kind of seaweed. The taste was heavenly.

Now, time to use this confounded cellular phone and see if it will give me a map.

The phone had more than a map, it had directions to the Levy household. He pulled off the road, and looked at the house overlooking the ocean. It was large, Nicolai assessed, but not overtly large. The house was very respectable and it did have views of the ocean. Nicolai looked over at the house and concluded that Adam and Gretchen were probably very well off.

He walked up to the house when suddenly he heard the shrill voice of a young woman coming from the back of the house. A young lady appeared.

"Excuse me," she said, "are you looking for something?"

"Da," Nicolai started, "I wonder if you could help me- I am looking for the man and his sister who live here, I believe their name is Levy."

"They're gone," said the woman cautiously, "were they

127

expecting you?"

"Nein. The name is Friedrich Nicoli. I was wondering if we could talk." He said.

"About?" she asked as she slowly put her hand out to his. He shook her hand, and she offered him a fake smile, there was something a bit odd about this man with a foreign accent.

"About some information they just came into, it is vital that I speak with them." He said.

"Vital?" She said.

"Absolutely."

"They're in Seattle, on business. Perhaps I should give you their phone numbers? I have them in my phone, should I call them? Or perhaps you would like to call?" She said, "my name is Rae, thanks for asking." Rae said sarcastically.

"I think I prefer to call them, put their number in here." Nicolai ignored her sarcasm, and handed her his phone.

"You're not from around here, are you?" Rae said as she punched in the phone numbers. "People that are from around here have manners. I'm only giving you their phone numbers so maybe you'll go away?"

"Just put in their numbers and I'll be gone." He said.

Christ! I came here for nothing.

"Yeah. Here you go. And I hope I will *not* be having the pleasure of meeting you again." Rae slapped the phone into his hand, then turned and walked quickly into the house locking the door behind her.

She peeked through the back window until Nicolai was gone, then she dialed Gretchen's number. It went to voicemail.

"Gretch, it's me, Rae. I just had the strangest man come to your house. He said his name was Friedrich Nicoli, and he said it with a strong Russian accent. Just giving you a heads up, bye."

And with that sentence Rae felt hands grasping on the back of her neck, and as her world slowly snuffed out, the only image she caught in the mirror down the hall was that of a tall, strong man whose face was covered in black.

129

Chapter 17

The plane ride was bumpy as Nicolai made his way into Seattle. He had to find Adam and Gretchen.

On the way to his Sable Forks hotel the clouds started to gather and rain. The castle- like hotel was made of stone and had large turrets, and narrow spiraling staircases. Nestled among a thicket of trees with the wide mouthed, slow moving river winding gently behind, it carried with it a genteel manner.

Nicolai was not intrigued by the charm, he now knew that he was getting close.

Adam and Gretchen had uncovered a few facts since their talk with Agustina. They had been following a cold case trail of copycat murders up to Canada. In every country there was a murder that happened on the heels of the last killing. Each done in exactly the same way, with enough time for it to be Hitler's entourage.

Adam and Gretchen could guess why Hitlers group wanted Agustina's father dead, for the new faces-but it was not clear why they kept up with the murder's that made a trail across Argentina, Brazil, Venezuela, Mexico and into the United States. The killings skimmed America, touching into Utah then Seattle then climbed into Canada. All unsolved, all with the same severed limbs with the scrawl on the forehead.

Gretchen had made up a chart on her laptop keeping track of the places they went, and who they talk to when they arrived.

"Adam," Gretchen said, "other than the first murder, I mean you can tell there is an obvious similarity, but the question remains,' why'? The police never have a clue, it's almost like somebody paid them to keep their mouths shut."

"It is strange. Ominous, almost." Adam said as he ran one hand through his hair, then suddenly grasping it tight.

"Do you know how lucky we are to have the Internet? In dad's day he would have have to have gone manually through the the newspapers and police reports, it only takes me minutes but would have taken him weeks." Gretchen said with a grim twist to her mouth.

"Do you have the paperwork from dad's work at MOSSAD? I want to go over it once more-I still can't believe that he really worked for them."

"Adam," Gretchen started looking towards him with a glazed eye. Gretchen started to cry and shake her head. Adam pulled her close, and in a strong, brotherly way he thought that maybe he was pulling Gretchen into an ugly world.

"Gretchen," Adams said that with a thickness in his throat, "am I being completely selfish dragging you across countries, looking for ghosts that belonged to father?"

"I'm sorry if I seem a weak to you, I'm not weak- I'm strong. Let me prove it to you. You'll see, I'm not crying because I'm scared, I'm crying because I miss dad. And if I can be any part to putting away the man that caused dad so much tragedy, *I will*." Gretchen stood up straight and pulled her shoulders back.

"Imagine what it will mean if we can prove what we already know- that Hitler was alive after April 1945. We can change history! Now, all we have to do is catch him, or his son- dad would be so proud!"

Adam put his finger under Gretchen's chin, and looked her proudly in her eyes. Gretchen was so right. Why did he even doubt her?

Nicolai checked into the Sable Forks hotel one day after Adam and Gretchen had checked out.

The receptionist working at Sable Forks looked curiously at Nicolai. She began to tell them that they don't give out information about their hotel guests, but stopped midway through her explanation and said, "Wait. It seems Mr. and Miss Levy left forwarding information. It says here that they will be checking into Prince Edward hotel on Vancouver Island in the city of Victoria." Her delft fingers clicking across the keyboard another minute then she added, "it says here that they want all information forwarded to them. It seems there waiting for a police report, is that why you're looking for them?"

"D- yes. I have information that they can use." He handed the girl his phone, then said, "enter the number in here." Nicolai

133

couldn't believe his luck. But then again, since when did he

believe in luck?

Chapter 18

"That's funny," Gretchen said as she looked at her phone, "Rae left me a phone message about a stranger looking for us. But now I haven't been able to get her back. Odd, right?"

"You don't think something's happened to her, do you?"

"Do you think I should have the police do a check in on her?" Gretchen's eyes grew round.

"I don't think that's a bad idea," Adam said, "I think I would."

Gretchen quickly dialed the police station at home. When she was finished, she spoke to Adam.

"So I spoke with an officer named Sgt.Moi. He said he would stop by our house, and then Rae's house next door. He said not to worry, though. Probably just a glitch with the phones."She looked as though her fears were allayed, but looked at Adam for reassurance.

"Yeah, I'll bet that's all it is." The frown line on Adam's forehead was still there as he spoke, Gretchen pretended to go along with this idea but she still had a tightening of her chest.

"Let's get back to work." Gretchen said with a lightness in her voice, "so this nurse were about to visit knew the doctor in question. But again the police report speaks of the events that happened that night lightly. So, any thoughts?"

"I have a few," Adam started, "same as you."

Gretchen typed a few things on her laptop, then turned it so Adam could get a view of the picture that came up.

"Gruesome, isn't it?" Gretchen asked.

"Absolutely hideous." Adams said with his eyes narrowing as they glided over the picture. "It mentions the nurses name, but again the police seem to close the case without trying to find out who was the culprit."

"Like us were about to find out, Gretchen said, "here's the house, or should I say assisted living condo? That's what the sign says it is, let's see."

Adam pulled into the parking lot in their rental car, and they both climbed out, with Gretchen clutching her laptop securely under her arm. They walked into the lobby, signed their names

136

into the log and asked to see Mrs. Waldgrave. The attendant told them she was in the fourth door to the left, then leaned back in her chair and continued to read her magazine. Adam knocked on the door and heard, "Come in."

Adam and Gretchen went into her room and were surprised by how much it resembled the cottage, not at all this sterile white room they expected. Mrs. Waldgrave was a spry, but frail little gray-haired woman with a lot of spirit.

"Come in," Mrs.Waldgrave said, "I've been expecting you. I'm having green tea, would you care to join me?"

"Mrs.Waldgrave," Adam started, "I'm Adam and this is my sister Gretchen."

"Yes I remember from our phone call earlier, come and sit down and have a cuppa." Mrs.Waldgrave neatly poured green tea into the cups she had readied for them. "Honey? No, oh well. I've been drinking 2 cups of green tea ever since I can remember- that's why I'm still here. The Japanese, ah! The people in some of their villages live to be well over 100. They revere their old

137

people, yes, such are the Japanese."

"Mrs. Waldgrave," Adam said, "we have from the police report your name, but it doesn't seem that the police did a thorough job."

"That would be because they didn't perform a thorough job." Mrs. Waldgrave said as she sipped on her tea. "Dreadful thing to have happened. Nothing like that had ever happened before. This was the kind of town where you could go to sleep at night without locking your doors. Not so anymore."

"So what exactly did happen that day in 1952?" Gretchen asked.

"That was a small group of people that accompanied that lady, Mrs. Brown as I remember. Yes, Mrs. Ava Brown."

Adam shot a look to Gretchen and she immediately got his meaning. *Ava Brown, aka Eva Braun!*

"This lady, Ava Brown, you said she traveled with a group?" Adam said as his pulse quickened. "Do you remember the other people? Did she have a son?"

"It's funny you ask that," Mrs. Waldgrave reacted to his last question with surprise. "Yes she did have a son, he was a lad of about six years old. She insisted on keeping him with her when she went into the examining room. You would have thought he was attached to her at the hips, the way she spoiled him. The rest of the group were men in their early 60s, and they all spoke English, with their rough sounding consonants, and the way they wouldn't use contractions,but you can't fool me. They all spoke German, but hid it remarkably well."

"And what about physical appearance? Do you remember what they looked like?" Adam asked.

"I remember Ava, I remember because I got all her vitals before the doctor came in to see her. She was about 40, she had a wide face and wavy light brown hair. She had put on may be 15 to 20 pounds, but she had a child to show for it." Mrs. Waldgrave answered.

"What about the men?" Gretchen asked.

"As I said, they were in the early 60s. The man who was her companion appeared to have Parkinson's disease. He was shaking uncontrollably and it appeared that he must've at one time been in control of the group, for the other 2 to 3 men were always at his side." Mrs. Waldgrave said, then she added, "now that I think about it the one tall skinny man called Mr. Brown, Himmler and at one time, something that sounded like 'Fuhr.'"

"Could it have been Führer?" Gretchen asked.

"It might have been," Mrs.Waldgrave said. "I was concentrating on what happened after Mrs. Brown's examination."

"Which was?" Adam said.

"After the doctor finished with her gynecological exam he sent Mrs. Brown for x-rays. It seemed he found a lump. Between the time he sent her for x-rays and the time we got the x-rays back, the doctor was murdered." Mrs. Waldgrave's lungs gave the collapsing sound of wind being knocked out of them.

"He was murdered in that horrible way, the police found him two days later, they came and took a quick statement from me and then whoosh! They vanished. The group of people and the police.

140

And it was a shame, a bloody shame."

"Did you ever get the results of that x-ray?" Adam questioned her with the intensity he now felt the bottom of his feet.

"I think the more important question is did *they* ever get the results of that x-ray?" Gretchen quickly asked.

"We did get the results, but they never got them, not from us at least." Mrs. Waldgrave said.

"The x-ray revealed, what?" Gretchen said as she gnawed her nails.

"They revealed what I thought they would reveal, that she had cancer." Mrs. Waldgrave said with a sigh. "She was sure that she was pregnant again. I remember she was talking to her son about how he should be very pleased to have little brother or sister to play with. I didn't have the heart to tell her my professional opinion. I do remember her son in the grievous look he gave her, it's like he was giving her the evil eye for even thinking of having another child."

"So they left thinking she was pregnant and not knowing that

141

she had cancer?" Gretchen said.

"Yes." Mrs.Waldgrave said with a look of exhaustion.

"Mrs. Waldgrave, with all this information you had, weren't you ever curious? I mean the names, Ava Brown, Himmler, the Führer- didn't you know that it was Adolf Hitler and his wife Eva Braun?" Adam said as he clasped her fragile hand.

"Why, no! Of course not! Adolf Hitler died Berlin in 1945- what would he possibly be doing here?" Mrs.Waldgrave said as she suddenly sat back in her chair.

"But from everything you remembered, it all seems like it makes so much sense. The names, the physical descriptions, don't you see?" Gretchen leaned forward, knocking her cup of tea over. "Oh, let me clean that up…"

"Nurse! *Nurse!"* Mrs. Waldgrave shouted. She pushed back the table and tried to get to a standing position as the nurse came running into the room.

"What in the good Lord's name is going on here?" The heavyset nurse said as she ran to help Mrs. Waldgrave. "What's

142

the matter, shug?"

"We didn't mean to upset her, it's just that…" Adam quickly said.

"I do believe," the nurse said in her bellowing voice, "that visiting time is over for today. You two can show yourselves out." The nurse helped Mrs.Waldgrave to her bed mumbling, 'don't do nobody no good, to come here and upset our patients! Lordy!'

"But we just wanted…" Gretchen started to say.

"Nevermind, Gretch. I think we better go." Adam interrupted her.

Adam and Gretchen walked out of the nursing home trembling. Adam gave her a questioning look.

"So she thought she was going to have another baby, and they left before they found out what it really was. What were they thinking?"

"The doctor's body was found over in the Miner's chasm, the gorge just outside of town. It had the same strange marks carved on the forehead, pentagrams and swastikas. There was also that word, natal or something..." Gretchen said with her mind spinning in a million different directions.

"Natas." Adam said as his mind was twisting the word to see what he could make of it.

"The report also said that there were signs of cannibalism, but I don't put much value that." Gretchen said slowly as if she wasn't finished talking.

"Why?" Adam said as he was about to have an epiphany.

"I just find it hard to believe that one human would want to eat another human, you know what I mean?" Said Gretchen while making a sour face.

"Natas is Satan spelled backwards!" Adam shouted.

"Why didn't I see it before? Of course, you're right!" Gretchen said as she pulled out her laptop and added the word 'Satan' into her computer.

The computer started making its calculations and all that it did was to make more questions to be answered.

Chapter 19

The next day Gretchen got the phone call from the county of Honolulu's police department. Adam heard her start crying when he went to her side.

"What the hell was that about?" he asked her.

"That was Sgt. Moi, he said they drove by our house and they knew somethings was off. He said it looked like a robbery, and that it looked like Rae surprised them." she looked at Adam with sorrowful eyes and said, "Rae's dead, Adam!" Gretchen said through her tears. Adam felt his heart fall to the floor. He had always been fond of Rae, he knew that she had a crush on him, but he had never been able to think of her other than in a sisterly way.

"Oh, God. Gretchen, I'm so sorry." it took a second, but then what she made it's way through his brain.

"What do you mean, *looked like?*"

"Sgt. Moi said there wasn't anything taken, t.v.s just knocked over, drawers spilled...but he said it was Rae that was reason for the intrusion. He said that they had the forensic unit dust the place, and they didn't have any fingerprints that weren't ours. It looked professional." she started to chew on her thumbnail, "I can't believe it-I can't believe that Rae is gone because of us! She was watching our house Adam! She wouldn't have been in danger if we didn't decide to go looking for somebody that doesn't even exist."

"But he does exist, Gretchen! You know it as well as I do. At least, he did exist. He's probably dead by now, and his wife Eva, too. But his son, you see, we have to track down his son." Adam gritted through his teeth. This was too much to deal with, he didn't even have the heart to tell Gretchen to stop biting her nails.

"But what about Rae? I've known her since I was a little girl, we were in Scouts together-and now she's gone!" Gretchen's tears started to come in droves, and she got the hiccups.

Adam grabbed her around the shoulders while she wept. He could feel her sob's turn into heaves. He didn't know what he should do, so he just kept up holding her.

Finally, when she started to calm down he suggested that she lay down and try to sleep, which was a good idea because in time her heaving turned to a restless sleep. Adam put a blanket over her, and watched as she slept.

Damn it! I can't keep bringing her deeper into this! I've got to make her stop, maybe she could spend time with Rae's parents, they could grieve together. I've got to make her go.

A few hours later she woke, her sleep restless, and she finally decided it was no use.

"Gretchen," Adam said, "I think you should go back and stay with Rae's parents for awhile. You'll be safe there, and I can go on looking for myself."

"No, no. I want to go with you, I was upset when I said those things before. I'm ok."

"I know you were upset. But I think that you'll be helpful back home. You knew Rae's parents, it'll help them having you there." Adam said as he was thinking of a what needed to happen next. "Rae was their only daughter, Gretchen. They have Chase, and he should be of some comfort, but I think we need to keep them in mind."

Gretchen lowered her head into her hands and sighed. "Ahh. I know you're right, but..." the frustration in her voice was unmistakable.

"There's no buts. I'll make the necessary arrangements. You're going today!" He said with a finality in his voice that she did not want to test.

"O.k." she said totally exhausted.

Adam was on the phone before she could finish blowing her nose.

Chapter 20

Nicolai looked at his phone with disdain. He knew all he had to do was to dial Adam's phone number, but he hesitated. He wasn't sure why, but he put it back into his pocket and grumbled, *'I hate this proklyatiye phone! I will talk to Adam in person or not at all.'*

He was on the flight from Seattle to Vancouver island, *At least I will catch him on the island.*

When Nicolai arrived at the Victoria's Prince Edward hotel, he went straight to the reservations clerk at the front desk and said, "I am expected. Adam Levy's room number?"

She started to type Adam's name into the computer and said, "I'm sorry. He already checked out-early. He was supposed to stay through tomorrow, but as I said, he checked out. Sorry."

Like a snake, that one! Always wriggling out of my grip! His mood darkened.

"Did he leave a forwarding address? Did he leave anything?" Nicolai said as his stomach started churning once again.

Her typing speed was not so great, and this time the lack of familiarity with the keyboard started to get on his nerves. Nicolai reached over the desk and grabbed her firmly by the hand.

"Listen here, cyka! I have been from one side of the world to the other trying to find this man! Now give me the information or I'll come over the desk and give you a free chiropractic exam!"

Slobber was forming on the sides of his mouth as the clerk looked at him with stunned silence. She broke free of his grasp, and typed a few more strokes and said, "It says here that his sister had an emergency, and had to go home, and he was taking an airplane to Dark Pines, New York. Here's the telephone number of the hotel he's going to be checking into. That's all the information I have." she looked more frightened than she had ever been—no one ever came to this island unless it was on holiday, and certainly no one ever talked to her like he just did!

Nicolai crumpled the phone number in his hands and stormed out of the lobby. He was so angry that he did not notice the clerk dialing the police.

Chapter 21

That afternoon the tall man dressed in black with the white hat tried to get to the reservations clerk, but the lobby was filled with police.

There were four of them, one behind the desk, and three questioning the lady. She was holding out her hand and grasping it with the other, as if to show them what happened when the Russian man was there.

I'll get to her later, then. After they've gone away-don't worry little lady, I'll be back. Then he zipped up his jacket and walked back outside without even being noticed.

*

It was rainy that afternoon,with the sun poking it's fingers through the clouds, it starting to drizzle on Adam when he went into the Dark Pines hotel.

It was about an hours drive North from Laguardia, and he

was feeling a hollowness in his chest as he thought about Rae and what Gretchen had told her was her final message.

'She said a man named Freidrich Nicoli stopped by the house. That he had a Russian accent.'

He was so deep in thought that until the car's horn shook him from his concentration-his car swerved, barely missing the other truck by a millimeter. He knew that thought's of Rae's passing was going to be hard to dismiss, and this near miss proved it.

Once checked in, he decided to call and see if Gretchen had made it home. The phone rang three times then, "Hello?" it was a man's voice.

"Hello? Do I have the right number? I'm trying to reach the Levy residence." he said worried that Gretchen had fallen into trouble.

"Yes, this is the residence. I'm Sgt. Moi. I'll get her for you, but you know she's sleeping right now, I'll get her if you want."

"No, if she's asleep I don't want to wake her. Sgt. Moi, my name is Adam Levy. Gretchen's my sister." he said, glad that he would now be able to answer the questions that were on his mind.

"Ah, yes. Adam Levy. I just dropped by to check on the house when I noticed somebody in the house. It was Gretchen. She seemed very upset about what happened to Rae, in fact, she was crying and she looked like she was berating herself for what happened."

"No! She was upset when I put her on the plane, but I didn't know she was *that* upset. I sent her home because I wanted her to stay with Rae's parents, not all alone at home." Adam said. The officer could hear the raggedness of Adam's voice, it was almost guttural.

"Please, Mr. Levy-if I may. She's perfectly alright here- I've been cruising by this house on my routes and I've put some more officer's on the route also. She's going to be o.k." Sgt. Moi said condescendingly.

"Correct me if I'm wrong, Sgt. But wasn't that house on your route when Rae was killed?" Adam said it as if it were a betrayal.

153

"So tell me, unless she's under 24 hour surveillance, how is she going to be *o.k.*?"

Sgt. Moi was insulted that Adam put it like that-yes, the house was on his route, and yes, Rae was killed-but now to be told down by *this* boy? He spoke again, his pride intact.

"Do you want me to get Miss Levy, or don't you?"

"Yes. Please." Adam thought for a moment, "Sgt. Moi?"

"Speaking."

"I'm sorry I put it that way. I haven't been sleeping well. This whole thing, the murder, has got my stomach all tied up in knots. I am truly sorry for what I said, I know it was *not* your fault that Rae was killed." he finished.

"Thank you, very much, for that." Sgt. Moi was placated, "I'll get her for you."

Adam now sat on the edge of the bed on red flannel bedsheets, then Gretchen came to the phone. She sounded like he felt.

"Adam, is that you?" she said rubbing her eye's.

"Gretch," he said, "I thought you were going to stay at Rae's?

154

What are you doing back there?"

"They had people staying with them already. Aunt's and Uncle's and such. Everybody was crying- Adam it was such a horrible mess! I felt so guilty being there anyway." Gretchen said. He could hear it in her voice as she spoke.

"Well I don't want you to stay *there*! Can't you go to a resort or something? I would feel so much better if you would." his voice sounded with desperation.

"I guess. But can't I sleep a little longer-I don't want to drive like this."

"Ask Sgt. Moi. I'm sure he would give you a lift-please, Gretchen! I would feel so much better if you ask him right now, so I can hear. Ask him." he urged.

"Oh, alright. Wait a minute." her voice changed direction, now she was talking to Sgt. Moi. "Could you give me a ride? Just to that resort over the hill."

Adam could hear Sgt. Moi in the background. He agreed. Adam could breath a little freer now, now that he knew his little sister would be fine. It was at this moment when he finally felt what his father had been feeling when he knew that his little sister was dying-that moment, fleeting in the air, knowing that you can't do a damn thing! He lay back with head on the matching red flannel pillowcase and felt a heartsick feeling for Gretchen- and for Rae.

Chapter 22

Adam had two things to do in Dark Pines, one was to talk to a man who was mentioned in his father's journal as being 'anti-American' and pro Nazi. The other was sleep. His dreams about Gretchen and Rae were plaguing him now, and sleep was coming at a cost to him. He finally got out of bed and went to the window looking out at what was a huge chasm that ran up the side of the small city of Dark Pines. There were gigantic rocks and evergreens jutting out of what seemed like a botttomless hole.

Adam grabbed some pastrami and Swiss cheese on Rye and gulped down a bottle of crème soda, and felt alive again. It was nice to find a kosher deli so close by.

Adam followed his I-phone maps and drove up to a large, lush estate. The gates had been left open and he pulled up to find a large man working in the garden.

"Excuse me, I was looking for..." Adam stopped. The man didn't look around at him. He tried again.

"Excuse me-*EXCUSE ME*!" he shouted.

"He can't hear you." a voice said from behind Adam. "He's deaf, and not altogether smart." said the man pointing to his head making circles with his finger. "Know what I mean? People call me Rooster. Like Rooster Cogburn from the movie?" Rooster said putting out his hand.

The large man continued working on the garden happy as a clam.

Adam shook his hand. *Rooster? Maybe he knows what happened to Rupert, the man who's supposed to live here?*

"Are you the man who's going to rent this place?" Rooster asked.

"As a matter of fact, no. I'm looking for Rupert Schmidt. He's is, or was, the owner here?"

Suddenly, the whole mood of the man diminished. Before he had been cheerful, now he became a man filled with distain. His posture stiffened, and his face got red.

"You are from the police?"

"Well, no..." Adam said.

"Then you get your sorry ass off this property! I mean it, NOW!" Rooster menacingly put a dog whistle he pulled from his back pocket and started blowing hard. Adam could hear dogs barking in the distance and he could hear they were getting closer.

Adam didn't wait to see what kind of dogs they were, he ran to his car and quickly backed out. Adam's wheels were spinning in the rocky dirt of the driveway, and he could see the doberman pinschers running after the car.

Later, when the excitement was over he went back to the deli and after a red cole slaw and broasted chicken dinner, chewed a toothpick in his mouth. Adam was pouring the last of his sparkling water over the ice in his cup and thought,

That was the weirdest encounter ever! Rooster seemed so nice at first, then he turned the hounds on me. I know now, at least, that I have to go back there-and somehow, I have to find out about Rupert!

He gulped back his water and left the deli and went back to his hotel when he decided he would try to call home, and make sure

159

Gretchen wasn't there. The phone rang and no one answered.

Good. At least she's not home. Now I'll try calling her on her cell.

Her phone rang until it went to voice mail.

Hmmm. She's not answering her cell, either. Maybe she asleep. God knows she needs it. I'll leave her a message to call me when she wakes.

With that, Adam fell back onto his double bed with the red flannel comforter, and immediately he was coaxed into a deep sleep.

*

The sun flooded the busy, crowded streets in Victoria, and the tall man watched the reservations clerk as she walked into the Prince Edward hotel. He was hanging on the fringes waiting for the throngs of people to thin. When it looked safe he approached the front desk.

"Hallo! Welcome to the Prince Edward hotel, do you have reservations?" she said sounding surprisingly up after what happened yesterday.

"I'm not staying here," the tall man in black said in a gruff voice, "I'm looking for information about Adam Levy. I believe there was a man here yesterday looking for the same thing as I am?"

Suddenly her stomach dropped. She could feel this man was more threatening than the man yesterday-and she panicked.

"Not again!" she yelped. "I told that man that Adam was in Dark Pines, New York. I gave him this number, *here, take it-please!"* and she began to cry out loud. Hotel guests that were looking at their maps trying to figure out their day looked over at her. She had written down the number the day before for the police, but now she was pushing it towards the man with fear in her eyes.

The tall man crumpled the piece of paper into his gloved hand and quickly left the hotel. He was gone before the hotel manager could catch him as he hurriedly followed him with a bat in his hands.

'Lord almighty!' the manager mumbled.

*

Adam woke late the next morning and went to the bakery next door to the hotel. The smells of fresh baked bread filled the air and drew him there. He finally decided to get a cinnamon roll and hazelnut coffee and ate them slowly, savoring the tastes that he knew was impossible to get the taste in Hawaii. He had decided to ask Rupert's neighbor for he had noticed a small cottage house directly across the street from Rupert's house.

It was not a mansion, like most of the houses in the area, and the chasm formed behind Rupert's estate, causing Adam even more to suspect illegal activities were performed in the past.

There could be all kinds of evidence dumped into that chasm over the years, and no one would even know about it.

A old man with a hump opened the door slightly with the chain still on answered when Adam rang the bell.

"Yeah?" the man asked looking Adam suspiciously.

"I tried to get your number..." Adam was interrupted.

"I don't have a phone. What're you want?"

"I was across the street yesterday, and I was wondering if..."
Adam was interrupted again.

"Yeah, yeah- I saw you. Your the one who drives that fancy
caw that goes so fast." the old man said in a New England accent.

"It's a rental," Adam said laughing inwardly. "And it's a
Prius."

"What do you want?"said the old man in his grizzled voice.

"Have you lived here long?"

"Grew up in Boston, but e moved here when I was about 22. I
been hera long while."

"My name is Adam." he put his hand through the crack in the
door. After looking at Adam for another minute, the old man
pushed the door closed then 'click' it was open and the old man
shook his hand cautiously.

"What do you want, Adam?" the old man gave him a long, interested glance.

"Do you know your neighbors, specifically the one across the street?"

"Can't tell you much. Only thing I can tell ya is the noises I've 'eard through the years."

"Can I come in? I don't want them to see me here." Adam said.

"Don't matta. They know everything that goes on around 'ere. But come on in, anyways." he said as he slowly gestured Adam inside.

"Nice décor." Adam lied as he looked around the boats inspired interior. It was dirty, and he looked around at where the old man was leading him. He sat at the kitchen table.

"Thanks. I did it myself. Used to be a fisherman, till I had my accident." the old man pulled up his pants leg and showed off his peg, instead of a real leg.

Adam looked with disbelief at the wooden leg, and said, "Oh,

I'm so sorry."

"What you have to be sorry fer? It 'appened before you was even born. What is't your lookin for? Is you a detective?"

"I'm not a detective. What is your name, again?"

"It's Jack."

"Jack." Adam nodded his head, then continued, "What kind of noises are you talking about?"

"Just loud noises. Called the police once, that was stupid." he said as he poured some scotch in a cup and offered it to Adam.

"Thank you." Adam looked at the pus colored liquid, and wondered how it would taste served in a literal 'dirty' glass. He gave it a sip. Jack poured out an equally dirty glass for himself.

"Why was it 'stupid'?" Adam asked.

"'Cause they came 'ere, not thera. The' gave me an 'ehyfull for botherin' my neighbor. Last time I eve' called 'em." Jack said as he emptied his scotch in a single gulp.

"Do you know what nationality they were? Were they German?"

"Imagine they could be. Don't botha them anymor'."

"I'm talking about in the 1950's. Was there an old man, a much to young to be his wife and a son?" Adam finally let loose what he'd been thinking about ever since he got to Dark Pines.

Jack rubbed his thigh, and thought before he answered.

"Ya'. There was a group of people that sounded like what you say. But there were mora people than that. There was a tall skinny man who was always by the old man's side. Helping him in his wheelchair, ya know?" Jack then poured some more scotch into his glass and twirled it around in the dingy light of his kitchen.

"There were some big men, brawny types. They had one son. I remember him because that's who the woman always had at her side. She looked sickly. But the boy would have none of it, he used to whine all the time. Him and his dog, a German Shepard, I think. He was always calling him 'Shatzi', I remember that one real good." Jack said with his eye's misting.

"Why is that, Jack?" Adam said.

"Because Shatzi ran across the street one day, the boy looking

166

on, excited. He ran straight 'ere and gave me this." Jack pulled up the leg on the other side of his pants and showed Adam a huge chunk of flesh was gone.

"Boy was 'aying, 'Good boy', 'good boy'. Like he was the fucking best dog in the world for biting me. I wasn't doing anything wrong, I swear. I was just working on painting my porch." Jack said as he gulped the last of his scotch.

He looked forlorn, then Adam poured the remainder of his scotch into Jack's glass. Jack gave him a ghost of a smile.

"Thanks fer that." Jack finished the scotch.

"Can you tell me what they would have used that chasm for?"

"Oh, that. We had a few kids from the city that went missing. That's when I would hear those noises. They could have done anything with those kids, and no one would be able to get to them. They say that it's one of hell's entrances, it goes that deep." he was sounding inebriated now.

"Do you remember when they moved away?"

"That was sometime in the 60's when they left. Just gone, just like that. But they always have people move in that were just as bad as they were, that man you talked to yesterday, Rooster's his name, he's their agent. Keeps a gardener on staff, but he couldn't tell ya nothing- he's deaf and none to bright. He lives on the property, in one of the guest houses." Jack recalled. "The people who move in always have their own staff for the insides. They don't want to be bothered."

"So you have no idea where they moved to?" Adam said lowering his head.

"Hear rumors. Hear them all the time. The girl down at the coffee shop tells me they moved back to Germany, to the Tyrol region. Near the Patscherkofel ski resort."

"It's funny you remember a name like that, Jack." Adam said. He knew that name wouldn't be a name an American could flip off his tongue. He suddenly grew suspicions about the man.

"I don't know what you mean by that, son. I have a good memory, that's all." Jack said as he balanced forward, trying to get up quick. But Adam got up quicker, and came between Jack and

168

his cupboard.

"What's in here? Huh? Let's take a look, shall we?" Adam sternly said as he held Jack with his arms held up.

He propped the cupboard open and inside was a treasure trove of guns and rifles. And a collection of Nazi memorabilia, plates, cups and long knives.

Adam looked at the frail looking man with utter disappointment. How could he have even thought that a man living so close to the devil could be innocent?

"That ski resort, Patscherkofel- you know they're there, right?" Adam asked.

"What I said was true-I did complain about the noise. Their dog Schatzi *did* bite me, almost making me completely disabled. *This* is what his mother gave me, to keep me from causing any trouble. They were furious with the boy for what he had done, but they never did try to reign him in." Jack said. He was now drunk, he couldn't keep standing any longer, and stumbling over.

"Don't hurt me. I was only going to scare you off-never to

come back. Trouble follows that group, I swear!" Jack said with snot streaming out of his nose. He looked pathetic.

"Tell me what I came to find out-tell me they're at that ski resort and I'll leave. You can keep that Nazi junk, I don't want it." Adam was disgusted. Never did he think such a man could exist.

"Yes. They're there. His mother gave me some money, too. In gold." Jack slurred when he spoke.

"Gold?" Adam's eyebrow went up.

"Quite a few bas, too."

"You have any left? Can I see it?" Adam needed to know exactly what this man knew.

"Ya. I have it in that chest in the mudroom. It's in thera, under tha floorbards." Jack sat himself down in the nearest chair. The room was getting dizzy.

Adam threw himself into the mudroom and threw the dried muddy boots off the chest. When he opened the lid he started to throw the galoshes out of the way, then he came to the bottom of the chest where he broke off the planking and froze when he saw the gold this man had. It had to be worth hundreds of thousands of dollars!

Adam turned to ask Jack a question when he realized Jack wasn't in the room. He immediately got to his feet and re-entered the kitchen slowly.

Suddenly there was an ear blasting rifle shot that missed Adam by a fraction of an inch, and blew away Jack's window. Jack stumbled again and shouted, "Get outa my house, NOW!"

Adam was in shock, and for a second he didn't move, he didn't breath.

"Didn't you hear me, son? I said get outa my house!" Jack was trying to be forceful, and he was doing a good job, too.

Adam shook his head to get it clear, and then he said, "O, ok, Jack. If you'll let me leave, I'll go. I'll never bother you again." he said as he started walking in short footsteps towards the front door.

Adam backed out of the house, continually looking around as to not take a misstep-he didn't want Jack to think he didn't mean it.

171

He reached the door to his Prius, and got in as fast as he could, making the car spin on the gravel in Jack's driveway. He looked in the mirror and saw Jack taking aim at him and heard another shotgun blast blazing past him.

Around the corner from Jack's house Adam's car rattled and started to sputter out. His first thing on his mind was Jack, but he quickly realized that Jack was a problem no more, he was a drunken fool.

Adam pulled the car to the side of the road and shut off the engine.

Crap! I don't know enough about Prius' to get it going again. I'm going to have to call for help.

Adam dialed information and called for a tow truck; it would be there in half an hour. He leaned up against the car, and pulled out his laptop-he wasn't a pro like Gretchen, but he could at least look up the documents that she had transferred onto his computer.

He was deep into reading a document from Mossad that had been released, but most of the names and places had been blacked

172

out, when the sound of a young girl said, "You just came from Mr. Jack's house, didn't you?"

"What the fu-You startled me!" Adam said not yet being able to see her. She was behind a bush where the fence was broken. "Come to where I can see you."

"I don't want to. Just listen to me, ok?" her voice was faint, but it was clear.

"O.K." Adam strained to see her, but he could not. "What do you want, little girl?"

"I'm not a little girl! I'm a grown up." she said sounding angry.

Adam did not want to scare her away, so he immediately said, "I'm sorry! I should have realized-you sound very grown up, now that I can hear you."

She giggled. Then she said, "Thank you much. I just thought you should know..."

"I should know?"Adam asked.

"I saw the people that rent that house."

"You saw them? When, how far back?" Adam's excitement

caught him in the throat.

"About a year ago. I thought you should know, since you asked Mr. Jack about it." the lightness in her voice was getting harder to hear, but Adam continued.

"You saw them a year ago? How do you know it was them?" Adam swallowed hard.

"Because I tried to pet their dog, they must love their dog Schatzi, because they named every dog they've ever had Schatzi." she said.

"How do you know what I talked to Jack about?"

"I was listening at the window. I always listen at the window. My dad gets mad at me for doing that, but I'm not hurting anyone- I'm just listening." her voice sounding pouty, then she continued, "I snuck onto their property, I know I shouldn't have been on their land, but I wanted to hear what was going on. They always had long cars with tinted windows driving in and out. People coming to their house who were dressed in black with red bands around their forearms." she paused, then continued.

"Do you think dead cats and dogs go to heaven?" she innocently asked.

"I don't know. Why do you ask?" Adam said.

"Because when they were here they had tons of dead dogs and cats, then they dumped them into the chasm." she said like it was a triumph. "They had lots of dead stuff. People, too."

"People?" Adam was aghast. "What people are you talking about?"

"Well I guess I shouldn't call little boys people. They can't even talk yet." she said.

"They threw little boys, dead little boys into the chasm?" he asked, his mouth getting dry.

"Yeah. But I know it was them because there was a man, he was in charge. He kept his mother with him, even though she was in a wheelchair. There was another man, a tall skinny man who was so old. He was next in line as far as who's in charge. His name was Goebbels. I heard the man call him by his name one night when they were having a secret meeting." she was getting

175

excited, so much so that Adam could say her eyes were glowing.

"Tell me more." Adam was walking towards her, getting closer.

"The man stood at the middle of the table, he stood and introduced the other men there. I remembered Goebbels name because they taught me that name in school. They were all Majors and Sergeants and every one of them came from another country. I made some noise when I tripped on a rock, and they sent the dogs out to get me. Doberman's, not his precious German Shepard's. His precious Schatzi stayed by his side." she started to cry softly. "I ran. I got away because they weren't looking for a girl, they were looking for men. I thought I was pulling such a good trick on them. But I ran as fast as I could for my house and I never told anyone what I just told you."

Suddenly Adam pulled her up by her arm, and she began crying loud. She looked at him with her childlike Mongoloid eyes, tearing like raingutters. It was easy to see she must have been in her thirty's.

He put her down and said,

176

"I'm sorry if I hurt you. I didn't mean to do that. I wanted a good look at you, that's all. You were telling me about the dogs?"

She dried her eyes with the back of her hand and said, "Yeah, I was. Well, they didn't find me. The following night was Halloween. My friend and I got dressed up, she went as a princess and I went as a pirate. We went from house to house, I got a big haul! When we went up to their house there was no answer, but we could see someone peeking out and they saw us."

"Could you tell if it was a man or woman?"

"It was a man. He was tall, and all we could see was a shadow, but you could just tell. When it was time to go home, my friend dropped me off at my house-it's the one over there." she pointed to a dilapidated cottage that you could not see from the road. Adam squinted to see the house in the dark. It was illuminated with a weak light bulb that had moths flying around.

"When she dropped me off she said she was going straight home, which is right next door. But she never made it home. All the people in the neighborhood joined in to find her, everybody

177

except for the people in *that* house." her story gave Adam chills. She continued.

"They eventually dragged the river for her, but you know there's really no way to drag a chasm. I *knew* they threw her body in that Halloween night. That is, when they were done with her."

"So you think they killed her?"

"I *know* they did."

"So all this happened Halloween night, last year?"

"Yeah. Their cars were from the Tyrol region.. That's in Austria, I know because I looked it up! Their windows were tinted black. The car with the big guy had a bumper sticker on it- one from the Patscherkofel- which is weird."

Adam thought the whole situation was weird.

"Why do you say *weird*?"

"Well because the rest of the cars were sleek, black limos, which almost never have bumper stickers. They had one big moving truck, one of those sixteen wheelers that had nothing written on the side. And as I said, the big guy got into the regular

178

car with the bumper sticker. I thought you should know." she withdrew and suddenly took off like a lightning bolt and dashed into her house. Adam could see her turn towards him under the light on her porch. She waved.

Adam stood looking at her for five minutes, until the tow truck came.

Chapter 23

Adam now knew that he was betting his life on finding Hitler's son, he just had to be sure he was ready to lay down his life.

Adam pulled up at his hotel and walked straight up past the doorman and clerk. The clerk yelled at Adam, "Wait! Sir- you have a message- they say it's urgent."

Adam had his brief bravery fail him once again when he received the message from the clerk. It was a note from Gretchen, and now he was afraid to open it. Adam was afraid she was in danger.

He immediately took the steps by two up to his room and threw open his door, still quaking as the note stayed unread in the palm of his hand. He opened it- it read, *'Adam, It's me, Gretch. I checked our messages at the hotel's we stayed at, and they had a message for us. They said there was a man looking for us- a man who fits the description of Freicrich Nicoli-the Russian man who was here to see Rae on the day she was murdered! Please call me ASAP.'*

180

He looked at the note and re-read it once again. Why was this man, this Russian man, looking for him? He hadn't the slightest clue, when his phone rang. He thought it must be Gretchen, and he answered it immediately.

But on the other end all he heard was, "My name is Nicolai. I think we should talk."

Chapter 24

Adam was stunned by the voice of the man on his phone. Freidrich Nicolai.

Adam was dumbfounded and mumbled, "Yes?"

"Where are you right now- I think I can meet with you if you're close by." Nicolai said.

"I'm in New York, but aren't you in Seattle? My sister said she had a reservations clerk tell her that you were there looking for us." He tried to keep his voice unemotional, but all he could think of was Rae.

"No. I am not in Seattle. I am in New York. I have been looking for you. As I said before, I want to talk with you, when can we meet?" The voice coming over the line was hard Russian, and not in the mood for play.

"I just got back to the hotel, I'm drained, to tell you the truth. Perhaps tomorrow?" Adam said not certain what he would do when confronted with the man who might have killed Rae.

"Why not now? Tonight." Nicolai demanded.

"I'm not sure." Adam finally got the nerve to say, "Why would I want to meet with you in the first place, huh? As far as I know you're the man who murdered my sister's best friend!"

"Who? That Hawaiian girl? I did not murder anyone! She was alive when I left her, and irate as well. She gave me your phone number and sent me off with a mouthful." He insisted.

Adam was befuddled. He was biting his lip when he asked Nicolai to repeat himself.

"I said I never laid a hand on her. If you do not believe me after we talk, then you can call the police with your suspicions, does this meet with your approval?"

"I still don't understand, why do you want to talk to me? What is so damned important that you'd follow me all the way from Hawaii?" Adam pressed his lips together.

"I have been trying to get hold of you since Argentina! I believe I can unravel this mystery for you. You can meet me in public, if you like. Is there a cafe in the hotel?" Nicolai offered.

"Yes, there is. I think it's closed, but seating is open. I'll meet you there. It's the Dark Pines cafe, in the Dark Pines hotel. I take it you can find it?" Adam's mind was racing.

"Yes. I will meet you there in half an hour." then he hung the phone.

Adam stared at the phone in his hands. He started to tremble. The only thing he could think of was to call Gretchen. She would know what to do.

Chapter 25

The time difference was to Adam's advantage now. It would only be around 8 o'clock in Hawaii, so he pushed Gretchen's number. She picked up.

"Hello? Adam? I'm so glad you called, there's a man who's trying to get hold of you..."

"I know Gretch. He just called me. I'm supposed to meet him in the cafe downstairs in half an hour. I didn't know what to do, I mean the man's followed me since Argentina! I don't know what he wants!" Adam's voice was quavering, he felt his stomach dropping to his knees.

"Calm down, Adam! You've got to get hold of yourself. You say you're going to meet him there? Are you going to ask him about Rae? I mean..."

Adam cut her off. "He says he had nothing to do with what happened to Rae. I don't know if I believe him or not, but he say's we can meet in public and then I can call the police if I don't believe him. I think I should at least meet with him, and I promise

Gretch, if I think he could have killed Rae, I will call the cops!"

"O.k., o.k. But then if he didn't...oh God! The guy must still be out there, maybe looking for you, too!" Gretchen words tumbled out. She was clearing her throat, as she closed her eyes.

"Me calm down? How about you? I'm more worried about you, Yeah, the guy might still be out there, but who says it's me he's looking for? It might be you!" Adam had to shout for Gretch to hear him. He continued, "I think you should get out of your resort room and down to the pool, there's always people down at the pool-he wouldn't dare try to get you there!"

"You're right. I've got to get myself surrounded by moms and kids, I can take my laptop down to the pool. I've got to take swim to get rid of this anxious feeling. BUT YOU! You stay in public with this Russian cat. I mean it." Gretchen said as she was finally able to relax. She didn't know why she trusted this man, after all, he was the last person to see Rae alive.

But if he wasn't,. *If.*

That was biggest word she knew, and she knew a boatload.

186

"I'll keep track of this Russian *cat;* You really know how to make me laugh, Gretch." Adam burst out at her joke. He hung up the phone and went to the bathroom to splash water on his face. He looked in the mirror and let out a huge sigh. Finally he walked down to the cafe, closed as it was, but open seats were readily available.

Adam chose a chair in the back of the cafe, where he could see the entrance, and therefore see this Freidrich Nicolai when he came in. The more he thought about meeting him, the more nervous he became. He started to bite his fingernails, when he started to laugh again. Here he was, doing the same thing he was always after Gretchen for doing.

The whole mood of the cafe was dark now that it was closed. Lights off, curtains pulled- it was un-illuminated and shady. Adam thought he heard a cat screech, that's when he saw the broken down body of the Russian man he had been so scared to meet.

Nicolai was once a large rock of man, Adam could see that,

but now permanently hunched over. His face was drawn and lined, covered in what looked like a couple days worth of beard growth. He walked towards Adam, and saw that look in his eyes- of an old man, no good for anything but a rocking chair.

Adam stood up and was inches taller than Nicolai, but he was surprised to find Adam quite charming.

"Mr. Nicolai, I presume?" Adam said as he grimaced. *Not exactly as I pictured him, but I guess you can never tell.*

"Da. I am Nicolai. You are Adam, I suppose." he didn't even pose it as a question. He carried authority, Adam could tell.

"I know why you went to Argentina, I spoke with Agustina. What I want to know is why you wanted to know about such thing? I mean it is too late to travel that trail, I have already have done so. What do you hope to find?" Nicolai asked Adam with bloodshot eyes.

He looked around the cafe, and asked Adam.

"Is there nothing here at this hour? Can a man not get a drink, at least?"

"Only water. There's the carafe over there."

Nicolai got up and walked over to the carafe and poured himself a drink. *Carafe? Ha! I will call it a pitcher, at best.*

He finished it in one gulp, then lit a small cigarette that smelled rank at best, then returned.

"You're not allowed to smoke indoors-that's a law, in case you didn't know." Adam said as the smoke went up his nostrils making him wince.

"I have been smoking this brand of cigs since World War II." Nicolai said as he took another long drag then snuffed it out on the counter. "You happy now?" he asked Adam with a shrug of his shoulders. Adam had never smelled this particular brand of cigarettes before, and the smell lingered.

Adam had his questions and he wanted them answered first.

"First, there's the question about Rae. She was a lifelong friend to me and my sister. Gretchen is back home right now to be with her family. How do I know you aren't the one who killed her?"

"This Rae, as you call her, was very rude to me when I was

189

there, but she gave me what I wanted without hesitation. Which was your phone number, so what good would it have done me to kill her, I ask you? If I wanted to get in touch with you later, why would I kill her, only to have me captured for murder?" Nicolai said.

Adam thought about what he said. It made sense. But he continued, "Then you were there within hours of a man who *did* want to hurt her, who would be tracking you?"

"That, I do not know."

"Don't you think we need to find that out, sir?" Adam said sounding young for his years.

It was the 'sir' that made Nicolai laugh out loud.

"I have always known Americans to be rude. You are *not* rude. 'S*IR*', ha!" He laughed out loud and slapped Adam on the back. Adam's suspicions of this Russian man melted away and thought of him in more friendly terms.

Adam allowed himself to laugh lightly, but he was still worried about Rae to let go completely.

"I, and by I, I mean Gretchen and me- went to Argentina to talk to this lady who was mentioned in my father's journals. He died recently and left us journals to read-about his life, and we were following up for him, for my dad." Adam said this as he put his head down. This was the first time he had talked about his father with someone new.

"Oy, da-I am sorry for your loss." Nicolai said.

"We found out something incredible, can I trust you with this information?" Adam questioned Nicolai about this when he realized that the Soviets have not always been kind to the U.S.

"Da. Of course."

"We found out that Adolf Hitler was alive past 1945. That he was in fact one of the people that Agustina's father worked plastic surgery on-and bigger than that-that he had a son!"Adam said this so loud that it rumbled, and he was immediately caught by this, and looked around to make sure they were still alone.

"Da. I found this out when I was in Argentina as well. I know it is big! It is enormous! But surely you realize that Hitler must be

dead by now. He was so close to dying in '45, he had Parkinson's disease as you must know."

"I know, I've thought about that." Adam said his tone calming down from the volcano it was before.

"I just spoke a girl who saw the group of them last year, and she didn't even mention Hitler. She told me about the guy who was in charge's mother, who I think is Eva Braun, she even told me about a man who might be Goebbels. She did talk about Hitler's son, so you see there is a reason for me to chase them! Can you imagine? Hitler's son!? Incredible."

"But we have no proof that his son has done anything illegal. So why must you chase?" Nicolai said.

"Yes, we do! We have a trail of murders leading from Argentina to Dark Pines! We have..."

"Yes, you do-you do have evidence of murder; but not by his son! Hitler could be tried for thousands of murders and we would win! But as I said, he is dead."

The room fell silent as both men waited for the other, it was a game of fencing, back and forth-one waiting for the other.

"Of that, I am sure" Nicolai said letting down his guard.

Adam threw himself back into his chair and covered his head in his hands. He let out a breath that sounded like his first, only it was full of disappointment.

"Look, Mr. Nicolai, I'm sure he's dead. But what we have here is murder after murder where the police have looked the other way. I don't know why it's important to me to find the murderer-it just is! Perhaps it's for my father, maybe if he hadn't died without telling Gretch and me about his life before I wouldn't care about it so much-but I do. There is one other reason I'm chasing ghosts, here." Adam sat up straight and started to flick his toothpick. "In every place we traveled, every one, mind you- there was a Catholic church very near by. I am finding out so many things I never knew about, Hitler's son, Eva Braun-Hitler, Goebbels and the Catholic church...I am telling you some kind of conspiracy is going on and I'm going to unravel the damn thing!" he hit his fist on the table and then there was silence.

194

"So your father did not tell you about his life before? Nothing at all?" Nicolai asked.

"No. I mean we knew he was Jewish, just like we knew that our mother was Catholic. But beyond that-no, nothing." Adam quietly said.

"Are you, yourself Jewish?" Nicolai asked.

"We're not anything. My father raised us to be very spiritual, but not to bog us down in religion. He always said it was horrific to be Jewish in those days. That it was better for us not to 'assign' a religion to ourselves, just to remember the golden rule. To treat others as we would have them treat us." Adam answered.

"I see." Nicolai said. "Back to the original statement, my country had Hitler's and Eva Braun's corpses taken from their spot of supposed suicide in Berlin and had them reburied by SMERSH in Madeburg, East Germany until 1970, whereby the KGB had them dug up and cremated and scattered in a river. They had them tested for DNA years later and it could not have been them-but the world cannot know this much. Now with the internet and the emergence of cell phones you can try to keep such things secret, but the Soviet Union *will* keep it closed! Do you understand me?"Nicolai suddenly became very militaristic, worlds away from the man Adam came to see.

Adam scooted back in his chair and stood up, nose to nose with Nicolai.

"If this is why you came, I'm afraid you've come a long way for nothing! Gretchen and I *will* let the world know what we've uncovered. We're not going to be intimidated by the Soviet Union or anyone else-I think this meeting is *done*." Adam roared as he pushed back the table, and backed away, taking small steps, slowly.

"Why do you do that?"Nicolai asked, "I am *not* going to kill you, if that is what your afraid?" Nicolai bowed his head to Adam and turned, then he reeled back again and said, "I met your father once, when we were both looking for Hitler."

"You knew my dad?" Adam was surprised at this turn of events.

"Da. I knew him. Agmon Levy."

"What was he like, I mean you knew him when he was young and idealistic?" Adam couldn't believe this. A man who actually knew his dad from his younger days. A man who knew of Agmon Levy, not just entries in Mossad's website.

"Idealistic?! Hpf. When you go searching in the past, you will find something unimaginable. You cannot hide treacherous behavior. All you will find is treason. You probably think you can still change the world- you cannot. You should let it go." and with that he was gone.

Adam could feel his insides turn to jelly and he brought his hands to his face and wiped the cold sweat off his forehead.

Chapter 26

Adam tossed and turned all night, dreams of Nicolai and Hitler

dancing in his head. When he finally fell asleep his dreams were

about Rae and about a talk that they had had on the beach when

he was 18. Gretchen had excused herself for a moment and he

found himself alone with Rae. He saw her head bouncing in a

good mood.

"Adam," she began, "I'm glad Gretch gave us a minute, I

wanted to talk to you."her chocolate brown strands of hair kept on

flying in her face.

"Yea? What's up?"

"I've wanted to tell you for the longest time, and I haven't had

the nerve to tell you- but I've had a crush on you like forever." her

small figure turning away he could tell she was blushing.

"Oh, Rae, I'm really flattered-but I think about you like I think

about my sister-I can't get past that. It would feel like incest if you

want to know the truth." he clumsily muttered as he was grabbing

handfuls of sand and letting them run through his fingers. The

198

blue of the ocean always made him think that there was nothing else so awe-inspiring.

"OH well, I didn't mean that we should *do* anything about those feelings....I only meant..." and she let her sentence run off like a soldier running for cover.

Off in the distance Gretchen was running back towards them with a small present in her hands.

"We got this for you, dear brother! Happy graduation!" she yelled.

He unwrapped it and inside was a crystal paper weight with a picture the three of them, arm in arm, on Adam's graduation day. He was smiling and had his diploma in one hand with the girls on either side of him. Rae's brother, Chase, had taken the picture, it was his graduation also, otherwise he would have had them all, the Four Musketeers, in crystal forever.

He was touched by the paper weight, and came nearly to cry- but he took a deep breath and said,

"This means so much to me. I can't tell you how much. Thank

you both." and he gave his sister a quick peck on the cheek. He leaned over to give Rae a similar kiss, but as she just put her hand out to shake, Adam noticed her quiet tears. She was heartbroken.

Later, they were having dinner over the counter in their home when Gretch started, "What happened when I came outside before? I mean between you and Rae?"

"I don't know what you mean." Adam said fully knowing what she said. He didn't want to get into a fight after they gave him the paper weight.

"I could tell. When I went into the house you were both happy, smiling-but when I came back I could see that Rae had been crying-now what's up?" she wasn't going to let this go. Adam surrendered.

"Rae told me that she had a crush on me and I didn't know what to say. I'm afraid I hurt her feelings by telling her that I felt 'sisterly' towards her. I can't help it Gretchen! I could never think of as anything but your little friend." Adam shifted from one foot to the other, nervous of what Gretch would think.

"Oh, Adam! You didn't *tell* her that-'sisterly', did you?" Gretchen's eyes grew bigger as she spoke, "I don't think there's a more humiliating emotion than to be told by the guy your interested in that he thinks of you as a 'sister'! Cringe de la Cringe!"

"What was I supposed to say? I know I blew it, but I honestly couldn't find my footing."

"I knew that she had crush on you, I mean she always said you were 'adorkable', whatever that means. But I never thought she would act on it. Personally, I don't see what the fuss is about." she punched his arm as she said the last, and it made him feel a little better.

"I'll talk to her tomorrow. I'll think of a nicer way to put it-deal?" he said as he put out his hand to shake, but Gretch wasn't going to let him go with a handshake, and she gave him a big hug. Only tomorrow never came, she avoided being alone with Adam, ever.

Then her murder happened.

Adam woke with the light shaft coming in his window. He looked at the clock and couldn't believe it was so late. 11:30! He jumped up and got into the shower hoping to make it out by noon, the hotel's check-out time. He had only one bag and hurriedly made it down in the nick of time.

He had the dream on his mind but even more troubling was his meeting with Nicolai. He remembered far too late that he had forgotten to call Gretch after they met. He picked up his phone and his battery was getting low, but he put in his call to Gretch.

It rang once and then there was a frightened Gretchen he didn't know.

"Why didn't you call me when you finished your meeting? Damn you! I've been just sick waiting and waiting..." she said as her tears started to come.

"Gretch, I'm sorry! Listen to me, will you?" Adam said as fast as he could. "I couldn't call you last night, I was....I'm trying to think of a better way to say 'scared', but I can't."

"You, were scared? Of him?" Gretch was biting her lower lip.

"No, not exactly. I had this feeling, in my gut. I wasn't scared of him, but rather what he was trying to say." there was a long pause now as Adam tried to think of what exactly had scared him. "I am sure now after talking to him that he didn't murder Rae, but then that means someone else *DID* murder her. A man who was *following him*. But he said something that has been on my mind since I met with him. Something ominous."

"Which was?" Gretchen asked.

"He said we should leave the past alone. It wasn't a threat, it was more like a warning." Adam exhaled deeply.

"You mean about finding Hitler, or his son?"

"I had the feeling that it was of a more personal nature. He told me that he had once met father, when they were both looking for Hitler." Adam swiftly decided to tell Gretch the whole story now, and to get her input.

"He knew dad? What did he say about him?" Gretch's enthusiasm quickly flooding the line between them.

"He said we should leave it alone. That's what he said, *we should leave it alone*. That's when our meeting ended, and I don't mind telling you that it's been gnawing at my gut ever since." Adam was glad he had told her, already it felt like he had two minds working on the problem, and at least as far as Gretchen was concerned, one superb mind.

Chapter 27

Adam was half asleep on his next trip to the Tyrol part of Austria. He was thinking about what Nicolai had told him, *to leave it alone*. This, he could not do.

The plane was choppy and outside it was raining below where they flew, and it was paralyzing coming to land. The plane went from side to side and then to a skidding stop as Adam finally was able to let the armrests go, he had his fingernails dug deep.

The flight attendant made an effort to make light of the nightmarish flight, and thanked them for flying with Austrian Arrows. Adam couldn't believe his ears and shook his head in disbelief.

He was able to finally get to sleep on the last leg of his journey, traveling by train from Vienna to Innsbruck. The clickety clack of the steel wheels was gratifying as the flight was terrifying. Outside was breathtaking, as a light blanket of snow was swirling around the evergreen trees.

It looks like a postcard, one I've never seen in Hawaii!

It was now four days till Halloween and Adam was glad to be away from the States for this one. He didn't think that he could handle the kids coming to his door and commenting on their cutesy costumes- not now with so much on his mind.

As he did now, Gretchen made him promise, he was calling her on a daily basis.

"Hello? Adam?" she sounded rather sad.

"What's up, Gretch?"

"Today was Rae's funeral."

"Oh, Gretch, I'm so sorry. Really, I am." he said sincerely.

"Dad was my first funeral, and then this funeral follows. I don't think I can take it anymore. I'm flying over to Austria to be with you." her voice went up an octave, she was not asking for permission, she was telling Adam.

"I don't think that's a good idea, Gretch. There's a man, and we don't know who it is, who's following Nicolai. At least he was- I don't know if Nicolai is still following me. But the fact remains- we don't know what's going on with this man. I can't have you to watch as well. I can't babysit you *and* look for Hitler's son! I think the church is involved, somehow." Adam told her trying to use his most authoritative voice. He knew it was a false shot.

"*Babysit me?* Who do you think you're talking to? I can't believe your talking condescendingly to me, I resent that so much! I have *never* been a burden to you, or your efforts to de-jumblize dad's journal!! You wouldn't even be where you are without my help, you baboons ass!" she shouted.

Adam chuckled to himself. He didn't want Gretchen to hear him laugh about the terms she used- *de-jumblize!* "You did get 800's on your SAT, right? Ha! Gretch, the irony is just occurring to me. I didn't mean it that way. I have to concentrate on all this stuff going on around me; I want to know that you're going to be alright, that's all."

"Nevertheless! I'm going to come tomorrow, I want to be with you. We're going to solve this together-got it?" she demanded.

"I got it." he said flatly deflated. "Bye."

He was next in line at small rental car company.

Rental car? More like rent a jalopy! He took the last, doorless

four wheel drive, and drove down the barely paved road to the

bed and breakfast on the edge of the city, Igls. It was from here

you could find the cable cars going up to the ski resort,

Patscherkofel. The crisp air crumpled his lungs, he never felt such

cold.

When he turned down the road and entered the parking lot and

he was awestruck! It was so beautiful he couldn't believe his eyes!

Coming from Hawaii, Adam was used to some of the most

beautiful real estate on Earth-but this was unreal. He expected a

sleepy little town, but had been awestruck by the beauty of the

snow covered Alps. There was a waterfall cascading down the

side of the mountain disappearing into the foam below, out of

sight.

Whoa! Was all Adam could mutter.

He took out his binoculars and immediately started to search

the vicinity as he rode up the cable car, but he did not have to

look long.

On top on the summit, about a half mile off to the right was a cliff broken off from anything around, was a building that looked like it was put there by God. There was only one way up, an aerial tramway going up the steep side of the precipice.

The tramway was operated from the shack on the top by some men in uniforms. He stood transfixed by the sight, watching the tram go up to the top only once, it seemed to be the one time it moved in a day, and he was amazed by the grandeur of the compound, wondering how they built it up so high with what seemed to be little help by the locals.

It was off to the side and other than a small shack at the bottom there didn't seem to be any other way to transport packages by any other way than by tramway.

The soldiers that came down the tram were ready to load their supplies onto the tram, and then after signaling twice with a bright light, traveled up the tram again. *'Very efficient.'* Adam said as he put his binoculars down. *Wait!* Adam noticed something else entirely- those weren't men in uniforms! *They were women*!

Adam was utterly surprised by the uniforms being worn by women. He had heard while at the university about how women used to fight along side of their men in WWII. But he never would have believed that such a thing existed.

He took another look through the binoculars to try and get a better view. Yes, the women wore their hair either short, or upkept so as not to touch the shoulders.

They all wore uniform caps and some were Officers while others were the obvious henchmen, or rather henchwomen.

But one thing Adam saw gave him chills. The fact that at the top of the compound was a cross, on top of a church building.

He had to get Gretchen's opinion on this turn of events. He knew that his phone probably wouldn't be able to get a signal, but he tried.

'They have towers coming out of the radio building, let's give it a go!

He was only mildly surprised when it worked. The phone rang and rang-no Gretchen. After he watched for hours, he decided to give it another try tomorrow and go back to the bed and breakfast for the night.

When he returned, he was so tired all he wanted to do was get a snack and go to bed. He walked into the dining room and he was unexpectedly struck with a feeling of joy at who he saw- Gretchen! She ran to him and gave him an embrace that not only was welcome, but was the best thing he could have wished for.

"Hello, big bro!" she said with so much enthusiasm that tears came out the side of her eyes.

"Gretchen! I'm so happy to see you- hey! Wait a sec, how did you know where to come?" he asked with mixture of disbelief and gratitude.

"I guess it was a good idea to GPS put on your phone after all!" she said with her right eyebrow going up in an excited manner.

"I forgot about that." Adam said frustratingly.

"Well, I didn't. I'll bet your glad to see me, aren't you?"

"Yes," he said hugging her back tightly, "I've never been

happier to see anyone." he grabbed her shoulders and told her,

"I have so much to tell you. Where do I even start?"

"Let's grab a bite, and you can tell me while we eat. I have a few things I need to tell you as well." she said as she grabbed his arm and laced it through hers. "Some major stuff!"

Chapter 28

Adam and Gretchen were finishing their quick meal and sipped on their cocoa. Gretchen said,

"Sgt. Moi returned to the resort I was staying and told me this- that one of his men had seen a tall man, dressed in black, leave the airport the day that Rae was killed. He noticed him because he didn't have any luggage, or had any kind of Hawaiian wear, you know, shirts, flipflops-nothing. He asked for a flight that took him to a small town in Austria, Igls. On United Airlines, for a start. That was unusual. No reservations, no luggage, he just shows up and leaves, like that!" she snapped her fingers.

"Why didn't he stop him?" Adam was floored by this information.

"He didn't know there had been a murder yet, and he had no legal reason to keep him there. So, there you have it! I gave Sgt. Moi the information about Freidrich Nicoli, and there wasn't even a moments hedging on his part- the man who was at the house and the airport were *not* the Russian cat." she finished.

213

"At least we know who it wasn't. But I told you from the night I met him, if I thought he had been the one who killed Rae, I would have called the police-no hesitation." Adam said with a hint of despair in his voice. It still bothered him to think of Rae as dead.

"There's a place I want to take you tomorrow, Gretch. I think you're going to be shocked, but we need to talk about it now." he said.

"What is it, Adam?"

"It's the location of their compound. It's high up, all alone on top of a summit, a mountain, really. They have a aerial tramway to go up and down, it's the only way. But here's the thing-I only saw women in the compound-blonde women in SS uniforms, black uniforms! I watched for hours, and I only saw golden haired women running the place. If they have any men there, they must be behind the scenes." Adam said as if he couldn't believe it himself, like it was a bad dream.

I know there must be at least one man in charge, the priest who must come with the Catholic church. Everywhere they had

stopped, everywhere along Hitler's trail, there was a Catholic

church.

He was finishing his cocoa when he stopped, and realized that Gretchen had blonde hair. If he could only talk her into going up- *NO!!* He chided himself for even thinking such a thing. There was no way he was going to put into such a dangerous mission. There had to be another way.

"You know what I'm thinking?" Gretch said sounding more curious than Adam would have thought.

"NO, Gretch! I *DO* know what you're thinking and it's crazy! You're not going to do that-there is no way I'm going to let you!" he said with his usual authority.

"And why not? I can find out where they get their uniforms, easy enough! Then I can mix in with them, and find out what their doing up there. You know your curious-how else are you going to find out?" she said twirling a honey-blonde curl around her finger. "Don't you think it's a major coincidence that I have blonde hair?"

"In the first place, young lady, I'm responsible for you now that dad's gone. I'm not going to let you mix with them to find out anything! One person, that's all it takes, one person to recognize that you don't belong there. Then they take you and do to you, *GOD! God only knows what they'll do!"*

"Don't start using *that* voice again. I have told you before, you're not dad! You don't get to tell me what to do. God damn, it! You really piss me off." she said as she polished off her cocoa and slammed down her cup. She lowered her head and breathed a deep sigh. She covered her face with her hands and then looked at Adam through her fingers.

"O.k. Then. I guess I was on an emotional high. I don't mean it-and I know you're looking out for me." she relaxed her shoulders,

"What do you need me to do? I'll do anything."

"Right now, I just need you to stay with me, I need that more than anything." he said as realized just what gratitude meant.

216

Chapter 29

Unbeknownst to Adam and Gretchen, Freidrich Nicolai was watching them with binoculars from half a mile away.

"Glupyye deti!" he said out loud, which translated to, 'Stupid kids'.

"Why are they trying to find what happened to Hitler and his troops? Do they not know they will only find trouble?"

Then the world went black for Nicolai. He was hit on the back of the head by a woman wearing a black SS uniform.

Back in the room, Adam and Gretchen were pouring through the information they could get on the computer. They had already read where the black SS uniform seen by Adam was the uniform worn by the battalions closely associated with the concentration camps of WWII. The SS stood for *Schutzstaffel*, which is the German for Protection Squadron, and started out as a small group

217

that provided security for the Nazi party. From there it grew into a powerful organization under Himmler's command. They were later declared a criminal organization by the International Military Tribunal and banned after 1945.

The fact that Adam only saw women working they found under the title, The Helfrin Corps. These were women who were more than happy to join their men by their side to fight in the name of the Nazi's.

"Well I'm not sure what their doing up there, but at least we have an idea of who we're dealing with." Adam said.

"Ooowwwww!" Nicolai's scream rebounded on the sick teeth-yellow concrete walls of the bunker in which he was held.

He was coming back to life in the most excruciating way-by torture, by any means.

He was strapped down to a table that clearly held bodies before, for the smell was that of death.

"Pull another!" one of the Nazi uniformed women ordered. She was a nasty looking pork pie, middle-aged, with silvery-gray with yellow strands intermittently throughout her hair pulled severely back and a cap perched neatly on her head. She was ordering one of her underlings to pull one more finger off the man. The subordinate did so, she placed the pinchers on the middle finger and twisted and pulled until Nicolai's finger finally tore off, accompanied by the spurting of blood, and his subsequent screams.

The middle aged woman had oak leaves on her shirt collar, and a silver head of a skeleton on her cap so she was of obvious rank and as she yanked up Nicolai's head by a handful of hair. She spoke,

"Do we have your attention?" she dropped his head so hard it banged on the table.

Nicolai knew the insignia well, This was the 'Death heads' squad he knew from WWII SS battalions. But what were they doing on top of the mountain in the Australian alps ? His head was swimming as it was aching.

"Da! Why am I here?" he was barely able to speak, his hand was throbbing and the blood covered his lower extremities and floor. There was a drain under the table, Nicolai had an idea of what this place was used for, and it made him form a trickle of sweat across his forehead.

"If you do not know why you are here, Got in Himmel, help you!" she said as she pulled up a large cricket bat with the Nazi cross painted on both sides.

"And they say cricket is a 'British' game!" as she whacked Nicolai hard across the head. He blacked out, once again.

———————————————————

The following morning the sky was dark as the sun rose on the gray day. Storm clouds dotted the sky in a way that reminded Gretchen of her art class. *'Push the brush upwards, Yes! Let the white peaks form as you continue to make circles with your brush!'* she could hear her art teacher's voice in her head. She laughed to herself. This did *not* seem real.

"Adam," she said, "So we know now *who* they're pretending to be, the mighty SS of WWII. But *why* are they here? What could they possibly be doing on top of a mountain, in the depths of the Alps? And what the heck is a church doing up there?"

"I'm not sure of the 'why's' and 'how's', but I am sure of one thing- I was up most of the night thinking about this-I'm putting you on the next plane out of here!" he said with a fervor that reflected how anxious he was.

"We're not doing this again-Adam, get used to the idea that I'm staying right here! Whatever you're thinking of doing, it better be for two!" she shouted as she pushed him back with the heel of her palm."Please don't make me get physical with you, 'cause you know I can do it-remember that time when I made you cry?"

Adam started to chuckle. "That was when I was five and dad said I couldn't hit you back because you were a girl!" he laughed again, "You're a real asshole, you know that?"

"Asshole or not, what do you say, whatever happens to you, happens to me-truce?" she said with her biggest smile, taunting him.

"Truce!"

Chapter 30

High up, above the clouds stood the mighty Monastery of The Fourth Reich, dedicated in memory to Adolf Hitler, now deceased.

"I told you that putting up the satellite system was a good idea! Ve are able to cover the entire area by flipping a switch. Now ve are able to continue the sacrifices uninterrupted." A younger woman, obviously pregnant, in a brown uniform said in a matter of fact way.

She was standing on the edge of the cliff facing the aerial tramway. She rubbed her stomach, she had been having pains.

"Vat is your rank?" the Death's head woman commanded. She had a pipe, which she was now smoking.

"I am sorry!" she said realizing her mistake. She knew better than to talk with an Officer.

Owww!, I should have said nothing.

"Vhat is your oath?" the Death's head woman barked again.

Puff, puff.

"I vow to you, in Adolf Hitler's memory, in Adolf's jr. name, as führer and Chancellor or the German Reich loyalty, and bravery. I vow to you and to the leaders, that you set for me, absolute allegiance, till death. So help me Gott!" the younger one belted out standing up straight and clicking her heels together.

"So, you believe in a Gott?" Deaths' head commanded once again. *Puff.*

"Ja, I believe in a supreme being."

"Vhat do you think about a man who does not believe in a Gott?" Death's head would not stop.

"I think he is overbearing, megalomaniac and foolish; he is not adequate for our society. Heil, Hitler!" she raised her arm at the precise angle and the younger tried the last to please Death's head, and it seemed to satisfy her.

The cold wind shot right through the girl's bones.

Death's head took a deep inhale from her pipe and walked up to the younger girl and said, "Very good. I am pleased you learned it all. And that little 'Heil' at the end? Brilliant! Seems such a vaste."

she said as she took one step towards her and pushed the girl over the cliff.

She yelled out, and her arms started to flail, her voice getting fainter, as she disappeared into the clouds. Death's head slowly exhaled the last puff of smoke from her lungs and walked away.

Chapter 31

Back at the Bed and breakfast, Adam and Gretchen had the look of exhaustion, as they finished reading the materiel on the Hitler women. They were absolutely light-headed when they were done and looked at each other with curiosity.

"So the women were a part of Hitler's plan all along? They have been fighting along side the men from the beginning? Why don't they teach you that stuff in school?" Gretchen sighed.

"I can't believe that dad lived through this hell-what's more, I can't believe that he never told us about it! Especially when he lost his entire family to those nuts!'" Adam said as he was pushing enter on the computer. "He was a strong man. A decent man. God bless him."

It was quiet, almost as if they were sending a moment of silence in honor of their father. Then Gretchen spoke.

"So what is next, chief? What are we going to do? Get up to that compound by flight?"

"I already told you, I am going to go up there, and your going to stay here. That way one of us can keep in touch with the police."

Adam proudly announced as he pulled his tablet out of his backpack.

"Did you get that before you left New York? Nice! But, how do you know they haven't got a foot hold on the police here?" she asked as she practically drooled over his tablet. "They have everywhere else."

She reached for his computer, and Adam pulled it away.

"Hey!" she said as her face turned sour.

"I'm not sure. We'll have to take the chance." he laughed as he punched her arm in a light tap.

"You really are adorkable, you idiot!" Gretchen started to laugh, but halfway through her thoughts turned to Rae. It was the 'adorkable' that got her, and she started to cry.

"I thought you were ok about Rae." Adam started, "Are you?"

"NO!" Gretchen said tersely, "I'm not. And I'm not going to be. I don't know how you can be so flippant about her. She was your friend, too."

"Yes, she was. And if we somehow succeed on our mission, we will find who killed her! Stay focused, now." he said it, and he wasn't exactly proud-but he said it, firmly.

"You're impossible!" she said as she got up and stormed out of the room.

Adam got up and walked over to the concessions room. He got a candy bar out of the machine and started to eat the caramel insides when he noticed a young woman staring at him.

She was a cool blonde girl with cornflower blue eyes, Adam looked around to see who else might be in her line of sight-no one. He smiled at her and to his surprise she smiled back. That's when he noticed her dimples laid across her firm Austrian cheeks.

"Hi." he said.

"Hallo." she said back.

"Are you smiling at me?" he asked as his heart started to race.

"Ja, I am." she giggled and shyly turned her head away.

"My name is Adam, mein name ist Adam." he introduced

himself. He held out his hand to shake and said, "Guten tag."

She giggled again and said, "You just said, 'Good afternoon', I think you mean, 'Guten morgen." she bravely held out her hand and said, "Are you American?"

Her laugh went right to his stomach and let loose a tide of butterflies. He was absolutely smitten.

"Yes, I am an American. Are you Austrian?"

"Ja." she said as her face flooded with color, she was enchanting. She looked to be around 18 years of age and Adam wanted to be sure.

"What is your name, and pardon me for asking, but how old are you?"

"Mein name ist Ilse. I am 18?" she asked as she answered.

That seemed to answer Adam's questions. He continued.

"Why were you smiling at me?" he asked.

"I was smiling at your eyes. They are beautiful, you know?" she said, looking away and blushing again.

"Do you think so? I don't know...they're just my eyes." he said as she boldly kissed him on the mouth. He closed his eyes and felt the tingle go right up his spine.

"Hang on," he said when they ended the kiss, "I don't even know you."

"Would you like to?" she asked as she grabbed him by the hands and started walking towards the stairs. She stopped, looked Adam right in the eyes and kissed him a long, hard kiss.

His insides turned to jelly, once again. He said,

"Yeah, I would." he said as she walked him up the stairs and into her bedroom.

Once they were alone, she rushed to get out of her dirldl dress.

Adam was taking his shirt off when he asked,

"Are you dressed in costume for work?"

"Ja. For work." she said as she jumped Adam with a sloppy kiss. He returned it gladly.

Chapter 32

Later that evening when Gretchen had come back from casing the compound all day with binoculars, she didn't find Adam in the room.

"Adam! I've got some news about the church atop the mountain...Adam?"

Gretchen looked for him but found no sign of him anywhere in the bed and breakfast or the ski resort or lift lodge. She finally went to the concierge at the bed and breakfast.

"I'm looking for my brother, Adam Levy? He's about 6 feet 2 inches and..."

"Ja. I have seen him. He went up to the room with one of the girls performing at the festival tonight. I have not seen him come down." he told Gretchen without looking up from his computer.

"Excuse me, but how would you know that? You can't see the stairs from here, he might have come down when you weren't looking?"

"I have ears. You can hear people walk on the stairs, and no one has been here, up and down that staircase. Except for you, of course." he said, still not looking up.

"Thank you." she said with a note of sarcasm.

"Tell me this, you said he went up with one of the girls who was performing tonight at the festival-what festival was that? And this girl he was with, who is she?" she asked him now getting flustered.

He slapped down a flier with tonight's date on the top, October 31-Halloween in America, Freinacht in Germany. Or at least one of the nights it was celebrated in certain countries. They even advertised that pranks would be pulled and children would dress up in costume.

"Who was she? What's her name?" her nerves were starting to run, and she was suddenly filled with horror. The people on the mountain could come down, in costume, and get away with murder. That's just what she was afraid of-murder!

She spoke with anger now, her heartbeat getting faster, "You tell me what her name is, and what room she is in, or I'll come over this counter and get it out of you! NOW!"

He stopped typing on his computer and looked up at her face, seething red. He had never seen a woman look so fierce before.

"Her name is Ilse Brown, that's the name she gave. She is up in room 4, at the top of the stairs."

"You're going to come with me, I might need you to unlock the door, or knock it down!" she said through her teeth.

He quickly grabbed the keys from behind the desk and followed her, close behind.

She walked up to the room and started to bang on the door.

"Adam! Let me in, NOW! Adam!"

The concierge asked her, "Why are we up here? Why are you knocking on the door? I mean if they want to be alone, who are we..."

"I don't have time to explain. It's very important that we find them. Or at least, that I find them. You will need to phone the police. Unlock the door, I don't hear anyone in there." she said with her heart in her throat.

He unlocked the door, and as she suspected it was empty. The room looked like they had been there, the bed sheets all askew- with a smearing of blood on the floor.

"Adam!" Gretchen spoke, terrified that he was gone. She was going to have to find Adam, before anything worse happened to him.

Chapter 33

Adam woke with a splitting headache, his arms and legs splayed, strapped down to the table in the darkened room. He looked around, trying to see where he was, but he already had an idea.

He looked to his side and lying there 6 feet away was Freidrich Nicolai. He wasn't moving, and Adam thought he was dead, but he had a small bit of life left. Nicolai looked at Adam and moaned.

"Ohhh, I thought I told you not to go looking for Hitler or his bunch. I told you it would only bring you sadness." he whispered.

"You're alive? Thank God for that. Have you found any way we can get out of here?" Adam whispered back.

"Of course I have. I have only been lying here for my health." his sarcasm was evident. "No, you stupid boy! There is no way out. Even if we could get out of these shackles, how could we ever get off the mountain?" he stopped for a few seconds then continued, "I suppose you saw who is running this compound?"

"I looked up the insignia, it's Death Heads from the SS. And yes, I saw they're women. Mostly pregnant women." Adam said as he pulled on the wrist restraint, but it was no good-he wasn't going to pull his hands out.

"How did you know about the Death Head unit of the SS? Surely they do not have libraries here?"

"Internet." Adam confidently said.

"And how did they get you-Mr. Know it all?" Nicolai sniffed.

"I am sorry to say it was a female's smile. I would have never believed it to be true, but I fell for the wrong woman."

"Is there a right one?" Nicolai laughed. Adam was starting to think it was true.

"I went up to her room, yes, to do what you're thinking. She must have put something in my water- and I'm not positive, but I think she must have hit me in the head because it hurts like hell."

"I can see where you are bleeding. There's a gash on the side of your head." he said thinking about what he should say next.

"My damn shirt is in shreds-now what am I supposed to do

when I go outside?" he wrenched and turned.

"IF you get out of here! Do you know what you are saying? Can you hear yourself?" Nicolai started to yell at Adam. Then he noticed the scars on Adam's back.

"Those are the scars from your scoliosis? Not too bad, I thought they would be worse."

Adam was immediately embarrassed by his scars and his face contorted in shame. "How do you even know I had scoliosis? Have you been watching me all these years?" he bit his lip.

"I have kept track of Agmon. You should be happy-most of the kids in my village would not ever even see a doctor, they would just live their lives, twisted and gnarled."

"I have always been ashamed, humiliated always. But for once I met a girl who would know nothing about me and the names the kids would call me in school. That's why I went with her- stupid, huh?" Adam looked away trying not to let even one tear go away, not one. "They called me a deformed freak. Even later, when I was better, I could still hear them calling their cruel names. I don't suppose I ever got over that one. I'll always be the freak."

"Listen to me, stupid boy. *You are not a freak.* Do you hear me? You are a strong, robust young man. Do not ever let them see that they got to you-are you listening? You will just give them more to hurt you- You must be the man who *had* scoliosis, yes! *Had*!! You have it no more. And you must remind them of the fact that you now have a back as strong as an ox, and you will take on any man who wants to take you on-at least, that is how we would take care of boys who called you names in my village." Nicolai finished, and with that Adam thought that he talked as if he *knew*.

Someday, Adam would have to ask him. But for now, he returned to the present. "I'll tell you one thing it taught me was humility. Never let me get above myself-it will bring me down. Always."

Nicolai moaned. He started to fade.

"Did my dad get out of a situation like this one? I wish I was as smart as my dad. You knew it, too, didn't you?" Adam said with a touch of sadness.

Suddenly the door opened and the lady with the grey hairs, leaf insignia on her collar and her Death's Head uniform pressed, held the pipe out of her mouth, took a pinch of tobacco from her pocket and lit up with a few puffs. She breathlessly inhaled her pipe until you could see the tobacco turn bright red. Standing right behind her was the tall man covered in black. He had shark's eyes, they were dark black without a hint of life emanating from them.

That must be the bastard who killed Rae!

"So you are Dr. Agmon Levy's son? You do not look like him." she said as she walked around the table and picked up the cricket bat once more, her pipe still hanging from her lips.

"Yes, I am. Who are you?" He asked, hoping she could not hear his voice tremble.

"I am Sofie Braun, junior you might say. Eva's my mother." Sofie said.

Adam and Nicolai looked at her, stunned.

"You're her daughter? Why do have her last name? I mean you

think that you would have your father's last name..." Adam mumbled out loud.

"My 'father' as you call him was a no good piece of trash! That Saukerl never loved me, he never even looked at me. It was always my brother...my brothers, who everyone thought was going to take up the reins of the Reich and be Gott!" Sofie spat and said firmly. "He did know it would take a woman to handle the reins of power. He never had the strength even to live." she walked over to the other side of the room and opened the curtains.

Instead of the light of outdoors, there was a series of specimen jars on a battlement that encircled the right side of the building.

Inside the jars there was contained a series of embryos from unborn baby status to what had to be dead bodies of boys up to the age of eight. They were all meticulous clean and shiny, little boys in formaldehyde, and had the Nazi cross on the background.

Adam and Nicolai looked with shocking realization of what it was- the boys that Eva Braun and Adolf Hitler must have born, and their eventual death. Sofie must have been the only one to survive.

"What is this compound for?" Adam demanded to know. "Surely you don't need to hide away like this-why are all the girls up here pregnant?"

"They are called The Bride's of Hitler. That is all you need to know." Sofie said as she puffed smoke, circled up to Adam's feet, took a long hard breath and whacked the bottom hard with her cricket bat.

"Ahhhh-0wwwwww!" Adam yelled out.

"Let the boy go, Sofie! He has no business here." Nicolai shouted at her.

"Let the boy go- let the boy go!" she mimicked him. She looked at Adam when her eyebrow went up the corner.

"I have a better idea! Shall I tell him about his father, Dr. Agmon?" *Puff, puff.*

Chapter 34

"I thought about telling the boy, too. But please do not reveal the past-I am begging you!" Nicolai pleaded.

"There's nothing you can say to me about my father!I know whatever you say is a lie!" Adam protested.

"And what if I told you about the great Agmon Levy, Ja?" She rounded the table to the front where she could look Adam in the eyes.

She laughed.

"About how he was only too happy to take his share of the Nazi gold to leave my mother and father alone? I believe he took hundreds of millions, most if it in gold bars. Surely, you must have seen it by now that he's dead?" she took a long puff from her pipe, then let it out in a long snakelike exhale.

She looked as if she were going to laugh, this was all a game to her.

"*NO!* He did not take payment from Hitler-*no fucking way!*"

He tried to wiggle his hands out, but could not budge them.

His foot was a bleeding mass. "Why would you say that? Why?!"

"Because it is true! I remember when he found us, and at first he threatened to turn us in-but then greed got to him. He could not turn away from millions of dollars. He took it as a payment for the time he spent in concentration camps. He took it for the life of his parents and I believe he had a little sister-ja, he took it as he said, *'payment in full!'*" she had said the last with sniggering in her eyes.

Adam turned towards Nicolai for help, surly he would know the truth. *Tell her, tell her!*

Nicolai turned his gaze downward. Seconds seemed like an eternity as his heart beat in his chest.

He said quietly, "I am afraid it is true, Adam. You should have gone home after I told you to, I said it would only lead to tragedy."

Adam's screams turned anguished.

"My dad would never, never..."

Adam's strength was leaving his body, and the fight he had in him was suddenly gone.

But he did see more gold than he ever thought possible, and there was the money that Agmon had left them, *payment in full.* That was what Agmon said himself, in his notebooks. The realization of Agmon's words rebounded in Adam's head.

As much as Adam didn't want to believe Sofie, he could not understand where the money came from.

Adam was amazed, dazzled and yet terrified. Agmon had left him and Gretchen more money than they knew what to do with- but this, what Sofie was saying, would explain everything.

"NO! What you are saying isn't true, I know it isn't-why are you saying it's the truth?! *WHY?* My dad was an honest, decent man who lived through the torture that your people put him in, the concentration camp! He simply wouldn't do what you said..." Adam continued to scream at Sofie and he looked at Nicolai once more for certain, he had The wretched look of heartbreak.

"Do you know he wasn't even a doctor? Ja. That is right, your father was a fraud! He completely had everybody fooled, Ha! Did he really think we would not do our own checking?"

Nicolai looked at the floor and said, "You and your foolish sister should not have gone looking for Hitler-yes, Agmon took the money, they offered it me, as well. I would have not have taken a dime from anybody who tried to buy me off!" Nicolai continued, "Everything she said is true, we checked him out ourselves, he obviously thought he would never be found out; I guess he was wrong. Wrong to try to fool the world about his being a doctor, wrong about the money."

Adam was staring at the ceiling, doleful tears running down the sides of his cheeks as he moved his mouth silently saying over and over, "Dad, dad.."

Adam felt his whole world crumbling down around him, and it didn't matter what was happening to him at present. Sofie's words were cutting into his brain, leaving nothing but wrecked bits of matter. Adam let out a blood-curdling scream.

In and out, he was starting to fade from white to black. Nothing made sense now, and even if it did, the terrible truth was one he didn't think he could live with.

Sofie was talking, and he was not listening, he caught the last words she said.

"So your father, he was not the goody-goody you thought he was, huh? The truth is too much for you, no? Let us get back to more pressing details, such as how do you plan on escaping? Surely you must have plans? Maybe your friend here has given you hope that you will escape alive? NO? OH, well." she took a few more puffs on her pipe and realized it was empty. She went to take out more tobacco, but realized her tin was void. She laid down the cricket bat and said,

"I am going to have to go and get some more tobacco, I will return. Come, Wolf." and she left the room with the tyrant, unattended.

"Adam, Adam...are you all right?" Nicolai asked.

Adam gave him a look of degradation. He never felt so ashamed of who he was before, and he was humiliated and never had he felt so betrayed.

"No, I'm not." Adam said tersely, "So you've known all along about my dad? Why did you keep it a secret?"

"Believe me, I wanted to prosecute Agmon for theft, that is what it was you know, theft? Taking money, even if handed to you is theft when you are talking about Nazi gold. All of it, is stolen. Stolen from the Jews, stolen from rightful people!" Nicolai was shouting at the end, then continued,

"But what would we have had to say in order to prosecute him? We would have to tell the world that Hitler was alive, that is one thing we could never do! Hitler is dead. I have the task of making sure that the world knows *that*. That he *is* dead."

"And what about the people that you meet along the way? What about Sofie? Are you saying that the world doesn't deserve to know the truth?" Adam said as his tears were turning to indignation.

Nicolai quickly sounded off,

"What have we found by knowing all of this? That dedication

247

to Hitler still goes on? We know that already. There will always

be those who are true to Hitler. It is like a religion, if you will.

People have to believe in Gods, from Paganism in the dark ages,

to Christianity in the present. Jews believe in God, and by a

strange twist it happens to be the same God Germans believed in-

but try telling them that-they will kill you for mocking their

beliefs. Surely you saw that every stop on Hitler's trail there was a

Catholic church?" Nicolai sounded as if he were in a line,

marching strong.

Adam shook his head, yes, he had noticed that very fact, and yet

he was not sure what it meant.

"There were always rumors about the Catholic church helping

the Nazis escape, and yes, I found out that very nasty piece of

business that connected it all together. Hitler himself met with the

priests in Germany, we have pictures of them shaking hands for

god's sake! There's been a line that connected them all together

from the beginning. Whether Hitler bribed the church or perhaps

the church thought of Hitler stomping out the competition, we do not know. Maybe you could ask the priest that lives up here, the one that runs the Catholic church up here?" Nicolai had spit coming out of his mouth, he didn't seem to notice.

"I noticed, myself." Adam said quietly. He didn't want to feel anything. He was numb.

"Why are we strapped to these tables? It looks like they're killing people up here. I don't get it."

"I will tell you why-you have seen these girls, these pregnant girls?" Nicolai asked.

"Yes. I did."

"They sacrifice the babies up here, on those tables that are smaller than these. I did not know why, but now that we have met Sofie, I believe I do know now." He said, his voice becoming darker with every word.

"Why?" Adam asked Nicolai with a sudden desire to know the truth.

Chapter 35

Nicolai's voice pierced the space between them.

"I believe they sacrifice the boy babies as a token to the Hitler jrs, over there. They believe it will give him someone to rule over, to be another god!"

Nicolai sounded sour, like he had a bad taste in his mouth. "It is what they have been doing along the Hitler trail. I do think they were taking lives until Sofie got her hooks into this mess. It was Sofie who decided to kill the boys only, it was she who put this compound on the top of this mountain." Nicolai stopped. He coughed up blood of a sickening color. After a few moments he continued. "You know that girl you told me about?"

"Yes?"

"She did require you to do anything for birth control? Well, did she?"

"No. She didn't."

"Because it was her job to get pregnant. Her cycle must be to the point where all she had to do was sleep with anyone who looked healthy. That would be you." he said with disgust.

"My god! Are you sure?" Adam panted, he had been had.

"I am never wrong." He coughed up red, sticky ichor.

"Then tell me, Nicolai, are we going to die?" Adam wanted to know the future at that moment.

"Da. We are going to die." he replied with finality and no remorse.

Nicolai was ready to die, if not here and now, then when? He knew death would come in the near future. All the pills, and what the doctor had told him right before he came on this mission. He preferred that he go out in style. Working a mission for his county would do just fine.

"I am not ready to die. I'm not. There's too many things I want to do-places I want to see." Adam was talking to no one, listening to hear himself talk.

Just then the door swung open, and standing there was a priest, along with Gretchen.

Chapter 36

"Adam!' Gretchen cried as she ran over to the table where her brother lay strapped down. She pulled on the wrist restraints but they would not budge. "I can't get you out, help me!" she said to the priest.

"You will need keys to unlock the restraints." he said as he pulled a set of keys from his robes.

Gretchen ran to get them but the priest pulled them away.

"This is your brother?" he asked.

"Yes! He's with me." she anxiously replied.

"Then who is he?" he asked as he pointed over to Nicolai.

"His name is Freidrich Nicolai." Adam said.

"Da. My name is Nicolai." He said weakly.

"He's the Russian Cat?" Gretchen was surprised as anyone, but continued, "Let him go! He doesn't have anything to do with this." she was looking at Adam.

"Does he?" she asked hoping that Adam would say that he was not involved, somehow.

"No. He doesn't. Unlock his restraints. Let him go." A heavyhearted Adam said.

As the priest and Gretchen unlocked Nicolai's straps, then came over to do Adam's, they were both feeling their injuries. Nicolai's head was crusted with blood and still bleeding, but Adam's foot was going to be an obstacle.

Gretchen immediately came to his side to help him walk.

No one noticed that Nicolai shoved the cricket bat down the back of his pants before leaning on the Priest.

"Come. This way." the priest said as he was looking over his shoulder to make sure they were not being followed.

The priest took them into a long passage with doors on either side. But he knew directly which one to go to, the large wooden carved door at the end of the hall.

"This is the one that leads to my church, it is a tunnel underground so I can go back and forth even during winter." he said so quietly that they hardly heard him, but heard him they did, they wanted to get out, now.

When the door closed behind them, Adam felt it was time to ask questions.

"Wait! Why are you helping us? Who are you?"

The priest made a motion with his finger to come along, and keep quiet even at the thought of leading the prisoners to freedom. When they made it to the chapel and crossed the floor into an office with large pictures of Christ and Hitler, which was empty, he began.

"I was hoping to get you off the mountain before we were acquainted, but it will have to be now. My name is Hanz Goebbles. And, yes, Joseph was my father. I was in the bunker the day my father and mother killed my brothers and sisters. I was the baby." the priest stopped, but it was obvious he wanted to continue.

"And no, I never told Joseph who I was-he took it for granted that I was a pawn-a priest in the Catholic church. I know how hard it can be to have parents you loathe. I spent many years trying to forgive them for taking away my family. I am still trying, I do not know if I can ever forgive them for the horror that they were part of." he was looking right at Adam when he said this. Adam understood he was talking as if he knew the truth about Agmon, he probably did.

"*You know?*" Adam quietly asked him.

"Ja, I do. But we will keep this between us for now. Don't ruin him for his daughter." Hanz said as he pointed with his eyes at Gretchen.

Gretchen was busy looking around for a way to escape down the mountain. Then she asked Hanz,

"Can you get us down the mountain, like right away?" her voice was quavering.

"The only way down is on the aerial tramway, we would have to get away when no one is guarding the machinery to operate it-I believe I can help you with that."

"Yes! I knew you would if you could, come on Adam and Nicolai, hc'll get us down!" she was filled with the buzzing of anxiety. Gretchen put Adam's arm around her neck and motioned for Nicolai to do the same with Hanz.

They were almost to the shack of the tramway when they heard the shrill sounds of sirens going off around them.

"They know we are gone! We will have to go faster, stupid boy!" Nicolai shouted at Adam.

But Adam knew that Nicolai felt badly for him, and his sister, too. He was trying to move as fast as he could, but it was not easy with the pain that was shooting through his entire leg.

Nicolai produced the bat that had caused them so much trouble, he was looking to use the Nazi crossed cricket bat as soon as he could, on Sofie the harpie, perhaps?

Chapter 37

When they arrived at the shack they pulled on the doors to let them inside. A cold burst of air whooshed before them. The girls in uniform who were taking their turn at guarding the station looked surprised when the priest stepped through first.

They pulled their guns and pointed them at him. Behind him stood Nicolai with his bat, ready to pounce.

"Hold it right there, Father!" the younger girl shouted in German.

"I am afraid you will have to shoot to stop me, my children." and Hanz stepped forward to the levers and started the machinery.

"Shoot him, you mensch!" the older girl shouted at the younger.

"No! I cannot shoot a priest! You shoot him." they were arguing back and forth when Nicolai stepped forward and swung the bat as hard as he could at both the girls heads.

'BAM! Whack!'

They fell down bloody and unconscious. They were both still

breathing when Nicolai started,

"You must go, all of you. *GO!*"

"I am afraid you must all go together, I will stay here and take my medicine. I am not afraid to face *her*." Hanz spoke.

"But she'll kill you! We have to all try to get away from here." Adam said as he was getting helped into the carriage by Gretchen.

"I don't understand, *who* will kill him?" Gretchen wanted to get aboard and get down as fast as she could, but she still had so many questions.

"The woman who gave your me and your brother these souvenirs." Nicolai said as he pointed to his head. "You do not want to meet her, *now go!"* Nicolai spat at Gretchen.

Now was the time to go if they were going to get off the mountain. Nicolai was roaring now, this was a true retribution now, he knew he would hit Sofie harder than even he thought possible-if he could just get the chance.

Hanz pushed all three of them into the tram and slid the door shut behind them. He stepped over to the main drive gear box and the machine clamored to life.

As they started the slow decent off the mountain they immediately saw the canyon open up underneath them, it was a sheer drop off the platform, all the way to the mountainous cavern 1,000 feet below.

Adam sat down in the corner and rubbed his foot as Gretchen and Nicolai saw Sofie come into the room with Hanz. They couldn't hear what was being said but they saw Sofie pull out a pistol and shot Hanz dead.

Then they saw what they never thought they would see, Sofie climbed onto the arm of the cabin hanger of the tram that coiled onto the cable line of the tram. She was going down with them, and they could hear her stomping on the roof. This was hair raising and frightening, and they all looked at each other in utter panic.

Chapter 38

"What are we going to do?" Gretchen asked Adam and Nicolai in dismay.

"Leave her to me. We have an appointment I mean to keep!" Nicolai stammered. "You must make sure she gets off the mountain."

"But how? I can't even walk, let alone save my sister! You have to help us."

"Put your *back* into it!" Nicolai winked at Adam, he knew the boy's back was strong enough. "You will make it. You must believe, that."

His head was throbbing but he could not get it out of his mind how he would love to be the one who killed Hitler's daughter. That's how he could go out-snuffing out Hitler's blood line, that would make his life complete.

The howling of the machinery made it hard to hear, but they could see Nicolai putting the bat with the Nazi cross in the back of his pants.

He swayed and you could see he was barely breathing, but he took a deep inhale and kicked out the window on the side. It suddenly became cold and windy as the window had provided some comfort was now only a memory.

Gretchen pulled her sweater up close to her ears as possible. Adam didn't know which hurt worse, his foot or the blinding cold that was now enveloping him.

Nicolai shouted, "You two will have to jump out when you get closer to the river below!"

"You're not going with us?!" Gretchen yelled at Nicolai. She hardly knew him, but she knew one thing-that he wasn't the one who killed Rae, and that was good enough for her.

"Nyeht! I will take care of Sofie, you two must get back alive. There will surely be someone to meet you at the station at the bottom, that is why you will need to jump."

"All three of us can jump, Nicolai!" Adam screamed at him. Surely he was not going to die like this-when they were all so close to getting out alive.

261

"Nyeht!! Take care of yourselves, stupid boy!" he said as he reached for the ceiling of the cable car and pulled himself up and out to the top.

When Nicolai and Sofie were face to face at the top of the cable car she reached for her pistol, but in that second Nicolai swung his bat with the Nazi cross and hit Sofie square across her face, breaking a few bones on it's way.

Sofie fell onto her back and yelped, no one ever had the nerve to hit her,

NO ONE!

She sat up as the wind went round her and she reached for her gun once again.

Nicolai saw her and reached across to hit Sofie once more. The bat came to a crushing blow across her face, knocking out a few teeth.

Sofie was covered in blood now, and her teeth were gone, but she reached into her pocket and aimed it right at Nicolai's heart.

She pulled the trigger and smiled when Nicolai flew off

backwards tumbling over the cable car.

Gretchen saw his body crumpling as it went and cried out as she saw him falling to the ground. She closed her eyes, this must all be a dream, or more to the point, a nightmare.

Now it was Sofie's turn to make them squeal as she turned her pistol downwards and shot a few times into the cable car, as it made it's way down the mountain.

Ping, ping!

"She's going to kill us! How can we stop her?" a grown up Gretchen yelled at Adam. It had only been a couple of weeks since her father died, but she had lived a lifetime. Now she was going to have to show Adam how she was *not* a little girl anymore.

"I'm going to stop her!"

"No, Gretch! She'll kill you, don't go!"

"It's the only way! Remember, I love you, Adam." she said as she knelt to kiss his forehead and pulled herself up and out the window.

263

Her hands were frozen immediately and she realized what a foolish thing she was doing. But she had to go through with this-her or Sofie. When she got up top she saw a broken bloody woman lying in her own puke. It looked like she was badly injured, but she rolled over and took one look at Gretchen and started laughing.

"Ha! This is what it comes down to? A meek little girl thinks she is going to topple the Fourth Reich?!" and she reached to get her gun from her blown out pocket. Sofie put up her blue frostbitten and battered arms to take aim at her, and Gretchen shook like mad, partly from the intense cold, partly from being scared to death.

Gretchen took hold of the bat that Nicolai had left and quickly swatted the gun away from Sofie's frozen body.

"You mensch; I will take you down with me!" Sofie said as she reached for Gretchen's throat.

Gretchen promptly put her hands up and started tearing Sofie's hands away. Never had so much been on Gretchen's back as now.

She was fighting for her life as well as her brother's. And she meant to win.

Suddenly there was a hand pulling on Sofie's leg, and she tried to kick it off.

It was Adam.

He was not going to hell for letting his little sister save his life because he was injured.

There was a moment when Sofie started to slip off the top and Adam gave her leg one more yank.

It worked!

Sofie fell off the cable car- screaming the whole way down. Then silence.

"Give me your hand!" Adam shouted at Gretchen.

Gretchen kindly put her hand in Adam's hand before she was pulled inside the car, trailing the Nazi bat with her.

"You're freezing!" Adam tried to be as gentle as possible.

"NO SHIT!"

They huddled together to get as much warmth as they could.

They were now getting close to the end of the ride. Adam looked at the shack in front of them and said,

"Look! Gretch, it's the man who killed Rae! The tall man in black, *Wolf,* she called him-it has to be."

Gretchen saw where Adam pointed and sure enough, she saw a man dressed all in black. She was angry at the thought that he would get away.

She screamed, "Adam, we're not going to jump! Do you get me? We're NOT GOING TO JUMP!!"

'Understood. We can't let that man exist. We are going to have to kill him." Adam said as he realized that it would have to be Gretchen who did actually the killing, as his foot was mangled.

They looked at each other with the finality of the moment, and they gave each other a look that made sure they knew who was going to do what.

"Right then." Gretchen said as she opened the door of the cable car. Adam moved to the middle of the the cable car and hit the light bulb out to a million shards so it would be dark when they entered the shack.

The moans and groans of the machinery were starting to slow down and the car was coming to a rest.

Gretchen crouched in the dark corner of the cable car and hid as the man jumped past her and went for Adam who was lying in the far corner of the tram.

Adam got a look at Wolf, The man who killed Rae, the man pointed a gun at Adam's face.

WHACK!!

The sound of Gretchen hitting him on the top of the head was deafening. The Nazi cross bat broke in two, and the man dropped the gun on the floor. There was a scuffle as all three tried to retrieve the gun, then there was a loud bang.

As Adam and Gretchen watched, the tall man in black slipped down to the floor, shot dead through the head, dead. Gretchen had the gun in her hand, and as she watched him sink she pulled the trigger twice more.

She looked at Adam and said, "I had to be sure. I had to be...."

then she dropped the gun and ran into Adam's arms where she

started to cry.

Chapter 39

Back in Hawaii, Adam and Gretchen were having a private memorial for Rae by sunset on the beach. They put a tealight candle, lit it, and floated it out to sea on a sturdy Plumeria flower.

They watched it drift out and finally went under when it was gently hit by a wave.

"I never realized how utterly gorgeous our sunsets were until I thought I was going to die." Adam said. "I hope that Rae's soul finds peace."

"You and me, both." Gretchen said, then added, "I hope her soul finds love." she paused, "You never told me all that went on in the compound."

"How did you know?"

"Because you've been quiet, real quiet ever since we got off that cable car. I can tell. You talk to me about sunsets and the such....but you never *talk* to me."

"Freidrich Nicolai said it best, he said, 'don't go looking in the past. You'll only find sadness.' I want to forget. I'll only be happy

269

again when I can forget what I learned. I want you to be happy, that's why I can't tell you."

Adam looked gaunt. He had a hollowness below his eyes and he had lost 10 pounds since their return and wasn't sure what to do with the money Agmon had left him.

"Is that why you're looking at starting your own foundation?"

"Wha- how did you know that?" Adam was shell shocked at this question. He didn't want anyone to know that he had finally found an answer. Especially not Gretchen.

"You still don't know? You never erase your computer-I can tell where you have been looking. But what I can't know is why?" She talked as more of an equal now, she had earned it.

"Well, since you know this much, I guess I can tell you this-I'm going to finish school then start my own foundation for the children of Jewish people who had their families erased by the war. I want to give them the chance to find out they had people who loved them, people who cared." Adam spoke with the stammering of a robot.

He wasn't sure about his idea. He wasn't sure there was still enough people alive from the war to make it worth while.

"The people from the WWII, I think they know that they were loved, by now. You're not sure, is that what you want to do with the money dad left us?"

"I don't know. I just don't know."

"How about this idea- why don't we use the money for children affected by cancer here on the Islands? It's a charity that could do wonders for kids affected today, not in the past. We could do a kind of Wish foundation, and we could start right now! We have all this money, why not do some good with it?" Gretchen's face lit up.

Adam stretched a smile across his face. What a wonderful idea!

He suddenly felt like his life was starting anew. He felt his heart start beating for the for first time in weeks. His father, Agmon, could have a purpose in leaving them the money. He had a lightness in his soul that started flying.

Yes, he would forever keep in his heart the appalling crime that his dad committed, and never, ever let Gretchen find out, but he finally had an answer.

"You're the best! I mean it, Gretch, I'm so glad that you're my sister." he said as he soundly put his arms around her.

"I know." Gretchen looked at Adam, there was a light she saw after all. And she wasn't going to let it go out.

Chapter 40

Back at the winter laden compound, it was like looking under a scab. Eva Braun-Hitler sat hunched over in her wheelchair. They were having a freinacht celebration, a little delayed, but festive, nonetheless.

Standing at the foot of her wheelchair stood Ilse Brown, aka Ilse Braun-Hitler.

"Ilse," Eva was talking to her daughter proudly, "are you sure you are pregnant? We want our line to continue, do we not?"

"Yes, mama. And I will take the Fourth Reich reins as my sister did." Ilse said overjoyed. She patted her round belly.

"We must get that gold back from Agmon's children. It is time."

"Yes, mama. It is time."

Now it is my turn! She thought as she pushed the wheelchair over the cliff into the abyss.

About the Author:

Leisel has been writing stories since the 7th grade and publishing books for four years.

She is a stroke survivor and currently enjoys life working out, and taping her Youbtube video series BooksRinMyBlood,

The 10 Things You Don't Know About:

The Harry Potter Series

Game of Thrones

Rebecca

The 101 Dalmatians

Flowers in the Attic

and more....

This is the series that compares popular books to their movies.